The Panty Plot

TORI ROSS

Contents

To A and P. Do not fucking read this until you're 18. I see you because
I see all. Drop it. Put it down. Go to your room.

Author's Note

This is your chance. Consider this a warning.

This is the raunchiest thing I've ever written, and this is coming from someone who once wrote a book called *All I Wank for Christmas* and had the balls to market it...in public.

What can you find in this glorious, yet quaintly foul, literary work?

-A shit ton (actual measurement) of references to dirty panties. Nothing is off limits.

-A guy that likes playing with his dream girl's underwear. In fact, let's just say the word together: Masturbation. There are a couple heated scenes of Milo enjoying himself with fabric.

-There's a period sex scene here. Nothing funny about that. As far as period sex, it's well done. (I may be partial, though.) If it's not your jam, you may want to uh...bail. Honestly, that is the least of your problems in this book.

If the fact that I included the words "period sex" in an author's note gives you chills, this is not a book for you.

I'm serious. I can practically see the reviews now: "Milo is disgusting. This author is gross. I'm appalled."

You should be. I went balls deep on this. All good citizens around the world should be appalled by this book, but I know my audience. I see you, and I glorify you.

Did I do research for this book? Yep. I even opened an account on one of the websites where you can sell your dirty underwear in real life and claimed the username that's in the book. My husband and I had some great laughs going through the registration process because I needed to know what was asked and how the sales website aspect of things worked. (By the way, I made up the glitter pubic hair option. That one doesn't exist. The others do.) I can honestly say that it was the most fun I've had while researching a book.

If there's anyone reading this that is on those websites, please know I'm not trying to shame anyone. I really hope this book doesn't come across that way. As Laney learns in this book, she can pay her bills and get out of a financial jam with money that comes from it, and anyone paying their bills and feeding their families is cool in my book.

And Milo sure enjoyed what she sold.

Still here? Awesome. We can be friends.

Kick back with a beer or a glass of something harder (because you may need it) and get your Milo on...because Milo sure gets his Milo on.

Much love to all my readers and happy reading! Now, let's get down this rabbit hole of depravity.

Fired

LANEY

"**I**'m sorry. I don't think I heard you correctly. Did you say that I'm fired?" I ask, my voice shaking. "Did I do something wrong?"

Dread sinks into my stomach, and I smooth my brown ponytail. Shit. Is it the ponytail? Do the partners think it's unprofessional? I eye my black pencil skirt and silk button-down top with a pink bow at the neck. I'm dressed appropriately.

My boss, a middle-aged prick who goes by the nickname Wayno because that's what his golf buddies call him, waves his hand like it's no big deal. "Laid off. We're downsizing and exploring artificial intelligence technology for some of the edits we require of paralegals. We need fewer of you now, and we just hired you six months ago. First in, first out, huh?"

He laughs at his own bad joke like it's no big deal for him. Hell, it probably isn't. He has a beautiful house in the suburbs, and the rumor is that it's paid for. His wife comes into the office every so often in expensive leggings and lips fresh from the filler needle. I don't think Wayno has any experience worrying about where the light bill comes from or paying his roommate half of the trash bill.

I worry, though. Lately, I've worried about bills a lot.

I tap my shoes against the thick rug and scowl around Wayno's office. He could pay a paralegal for a year for the price of furnishing this small room. Brass, kitschy objects line his desk, and expensive pens sit in the blotter. A painting I'm reasonably sure is a Picasso hangs on the wall above a small bar cart cluttered with top-shelf liquor bottles. His own suit costs a month's rent.

"What about research and hunting down witnesses? Can artificial intelligence do that?"

Wayno frowns and looks at his desk. "Uh, not yet, but technology is always evolving these days. We have five other paralegals, though. They can handle that workload."

I swallow, but it's a dry gulp. My mouth feels like cotton. Ironically, my hands sweat like I'm holding on to the edge of a cliff for dear life.

The only thing I'm holding onto is the cliff of financial ruin.

I had an accident a little over a year ago and not many people know about the scar that runs up my entire leg. It's faded enough to wear a bathing suit without giving it a second thought. What hasn't faded is the ninety-thousand-dollar hospital bill for two broken femurs and a gash large enough on my leg that I had to be airlifted out of the ski resort because people thought I had bled to death. It took three pints of blood to replace what I lost when a branch caught me on the way down. I hadn't yet been hired by the firm, and my parents didn't have me on their insurance because I was too old. The hospital system allows payments, but between medical bills, payments for a small student loan for my community college degree in paralegal studies, rent, food, utilities, and a car payment for a humble Honda with its fair share of miles on it, I'm already toeing the line toward medical bankruptcy.

I squeeze my eyes shut, willing the tears not to fall. I can get another paralegal job. I'm good at what I do. But I live in a small suburb, so it'll mean looking in nearby Minneapolis. That means a longer commute and more gas or just up and moving to a more expensive city.

It could also take me months to find something.

Time is something I don't have. I already survive on canned soup and homemade tuna sandwiches. I limit how much I go out with my friends, choosing house parties and potlucks over big bar nights. Sure, I may go out for a beer, but I only get *one* beer, making sure it's the nightly special. More than one bartender has given me side eye for paying with quarters. It's not like I go crazy with expensive brunches, rounds of drinks, and long vacations. In fact, I haven't been on vacation since the skiing incident. Part of that is finances. Part of that is fear of being airlifted out of a situation and paying the airlift fee. That wasn't cheap.

My salary goes to pay what I can on the medical bill, pay off my school loan as fast as I can, and pay Chantel, my roommate, half the rent and utilities on our two-bedroom bungalow.

"I'll give you a nice letter of recommendation," Wayno says, jolting me out of my thoughts of dollar signs and just getting it over with and filing for bankruptcy. That will negatively impact my credit, and I can take buying a new car or a house off the list in the next seven years. He crosses his feet on top of his desk and temples his fingers under his graying goatee. The goatee is an inch past his chin, and I watch him idly stroke it with a finger. I've always found it funny that he does that. Maybe he likes feeling the hair. Lord knows he doesn't have much on his head. "You'll find something and will be right as rain in a few months."

Right as rain? Doesn't this dipshit know that a lot of people are two missed paychecks away from the streets? Sure, I don't see Chantel tossing me out on the street with an oversized shipping box and the clothes on my back, but she has her own bills to pay. We're in a housing crisis, and there would be a line up the sidewalk if she advertised for a roommate at a bungalow with a porch swing and backyard fire pit.

I mentally run through the list of places to get a job until I find another paralegal gig. I could work at the local Target, waitress at the pizza joint near my house to save on commuting gas, or see if the library needs someone to shelve books on weekends. I could do meal delivery or work for one of those shopping apps in between...and still come up short every month.

I look at the ceiling and will the tears not to flow as I listen to Wayno walk me through how I need to box up my things because they're walking me out today to avoid a disgruntled employee fucking around with client information. What kind of psycho does he think I am? Most of the clients I work with are pro bono cases that don't have people in their corner. I would never take anything out on them. But there's no use trying to convince him of that. I'm sure it's company policy, and they've heard excuses before.

He talks me through how I'll hear from human resources soon about COBRA insurance I can't afford anyway and confirms my personal email on file to send the letter of reference. They'll pay me my two accrued vacation days and a week's pay for severance, which won't get me far. They may as well sign it over to Sisters of Mercy Hospital.

I open my mouth to talk but nothing comes out. All I can do is stand, smooth my skirt, and let him lead me to his office door by my elbow where Gill, our floor's security guard, stands with a sad smile and a box.

Gill silently walks me to my desk and waits with me while I pack up my picture frames of my parents and a few odds and ends like tampons, gum, and a pair of cheap walking shoes I use to walk around the building on my lunch hours since expensive gym memberships are out of my league. I stare at a picture of my parents before wiping a smidge of dust from the frame and placing it in my sad packing box. I could ask them for a little money, but I didn't grow up rich. They live on a shoestring budget since Dad had to take early retirement due to his arthritis. Mom still works, but it's tight, hence them not being able to help with my community college degree. They're good for a dinner or two once a week with vegetables and fresh fruit and would let me move back home if it came down to it. But I'm twenty-eight with a two-year degree and the ability to work. My parents come from a different time when housing was less expensive and degrees were worth something. They have medical insurance. I'm too old to be on their plan. They grew up without empathy for moving back home or even living at home without paying rent after eighteen.

Personally, I'm not sure they'd last five minutes as a millennial or member of Gen Z, but that's just me. Mom always laughs that I wouldn't have lasted five minutes in 1975, so it goes both ways.

"What the fuck is happening?" a voice asks. Gill adjusts his belt like he's preparing for a fight while my coworker and close friend, Samantha Hillis, glares at him from the entrance to my cubicle like the whole thing is his fault.

She doesn't move. She simply stands in the doorway, both hands braced against the frame that wobbles a bit as she grips the sides until her knuckles turn white. She breathes through her nostrils like a charging bull. Her curly, red hair is in a low messy bun, and some tendrils have popped free, giving her the illusion of a mad woman. Her ice-blue eyes squint at Gill, and her naturally thick upper lip curls.

"I'm toast," I say, not recognizing my voice. It's husky and full of fear for the future and shame at my coworkers seeing me pack up my stuff like I did something wrong. "I'll text you later."

"That piece of shit!" she says louder than she should. If people hadn't noticed I was quietly packing, they know now. Typing stops in nearby cubicles, and I can practically feel people turn an ear in our direction.

"Shh. No use two of us getting shit canned today," I say, putting my finger to my lips. Samantha is Wayno's administrative assistant. Honestly, I'm surprised she didn't already know about this. The look on her face says it's a surprise to her, though. "I'm packing up, but we'll talk about it later."

"No, queen. You'll go out for drinks tonight. I won't take no for an answer. We need to plan on your job search and get you shitfaced."

"I can't afford it, Sam," I mumble, looking at my old desk and finally letting a tear run down my cheek. Gill reaches into my tissue box and hands me one. I give him a kind smile before remembering that the tissues are mine. I put the box in the packing container on top of my shoes. "I'm out of a job when things were tight before."

"My treat. We'll grab Chantel and talk through bills, drink more than a few, and maybe even get you laid."

Gill stiffens and reddens next to me. His mouth flops open a little like a fish, and Samantha gives him a dirty look. "You don't think she needs a good lay after getting shit canned, Gill?" Samantha asks.

"I don't know how to answer that," Gills says, looking between Samantha and me like he would like to be anywhere else but in this conversation. "I feel awkward."

Samantha points her finger in my face, and I stare at it, probably crossing my eyes as I examine her perfectly manicured nail. "We're going to get you drunk, and we're going to get you laid by the hottest guy we can find. Want me to call your brother?"

"My Lord," Gill says under his breath next to me, and my eyes widen.

"She doesn't mean I'm going to get laid by my brother!" I clarify quickly, waving my hands in front of my face.

"Get your mind out of the gutter, Gill. Her brother has the hottest best friend known to mankind." Samantha gives a little swoon, bringing her hand to her forehead like she's an actress in *Gone with the Wind,* and leans against the beige cabinet by the doorway. "Milo Coulson."

Milo Coulson. Just the name makes my clit tingle. I've been in love – er, lust – with the bastard since I was a freshman in high school and he was a senior. I'd like to say he was just a stupid crush I had to see at school, but no such luck.

He's my brother's ride-or-die best friend and was always at my house when I was going through puberty. I remember coming home with tears in my eyes from getting braces the summer after freshman year and wanting ice cream to help soothe my mouth pain. I walked into the kitchen, and there was a dripping-wet and shirtless Milo eating *my* pistachio ice cream straight from the carton with a spoon. He held it out to me and asked if I wanted to share, but it was hard to concentrate on anything with drops of water running down his perfect chest and stomach.

Unfortunately, shit like that was always happening. My brother and Milo playing with the garden hose on summer days. Milo spending the night, sleeping in a pair of tight boxer briefs, and walking past me to the bathroom in the morning while sporting humongous morning wood. Milo coming to the table to eat my mother's cinnamon rolls in the morning with tousled hair that looked like he'd been fucked three different ways.

He's sex on a stick, and the first time I had an orgasm was with my detachable shower head while thinking about what it would be like to shower with him at my back and lathering soap on my ass cheeks.

I was awkward and gangly in high school while he was a god of sexual pleasure. He drowned in pussy and tits, even having two dates to prom before polyamory was a thing. He was gorgeous and funny. Everyone loved him as captain of the basketball team, especially when he won state junior year. He was Captain Von Trapp in the spring production of *The Sound of Music* senior year and killed it until my brother dared him to sing "Anal Vice" instead of "Edelweiss."

The crowd broke up with laughter, the principal charged the stage, and he got three days of suspension. It didn't matter grade-wise, though. By that time, he already had his acceptance to Minnesota State where he majored in finance.

Now, Milo Coulson drives a BMW and has a great job in Minneapolis at a hedge fund company. He shares a pimped-out condo with my brother, not because they can't afford a place for their respective selves, but because they enjoy being roommates. They're both dedicated bachelors at the age of thirty-one, and there's no shortage of women coming through the place. They may as well put in a revolving front door.

He has dark hair that's always cut into the current style, high cheekbones any woman would envy, luscious lips, long eyelashes, and movie star shoulders. Given how perfect he is, it's reasonable to guess that his dick pisses diamond bracelets and tastes like a chocolate bar.

"No! I do not need you to call Landon and drag Milo out to a bar so we can drool over him. I'm embarrassed, and I want to feel sorry for myself without worrying if my face looks weird."

"Fine," she says with a devious smile. I know that grin, and it will definitely not be fine. She's going to call him. She's going to complain to Landon, tell him his sister got fired, and demand that he drag Milo out to the bar so they can all witness one of the worst moments of my adult life. "You're going out. That's final."

Drinks on a Tuesday

MILO

"Could she describe the taste of your balls during a police lineup situation?" Landon asks, setting the beer bucket on the table between us and sliding into the chair across from me.

I grab a bottle from the bucket, squint at the label of whatever pretentious beer my best friend insisted on getting this time, and take a swig before answering. "I dropped her off at her door like a gentleman. She wasn't my type. Besides, would the police ever line up guys and have women taste their balls for identification?"

Landon furrows his brow and leans back like he's shocked I don't find his joke funny. "What's up with you lately? That's the third Tinder date you've been on without your dick going into at least one hole. Do you have crabs or something?"

"Yes, that's it. I have crabs and want to save the women of the greater Minneapolis area from weeks of itchy crotch. Did you ever think that maybe I'm just getting too old for this dating around and fucking for fun shit?"

"Will it ever *not* be fun to fuck?"

"OK, it's fun to fuck, but I'd like to start putting myself in situations where I remember their names when I run into them at the grocery store a month later. Hell, do you remember what happened last February?"

My best friend cringes. "There's no way you could have known that woman was married."

"I would have liked to have found out before her husband came home early from a business trip while I had my dick in one hole and her favorite dildo in the other."

Landon chuckles and leans forward in his seat just as the waitress arrives with his pot roast sandwich with fries and a buffalo chicken sandwich with jalapeno poppers for me. I stare at the plate for a few seconds before tentatively reaching for a popper. Sigh. More bar food.

Beer. Fatty junk food. Women that ride my dick at night, never to be seen again. Living with my best friend. I'm thirty-one and successful in my career. It's fun to go out with different women and party like I did when I was twenty-three, but there's been something missing lately. I stay awake on the nights I happen to be alone and think about it. I know what I'm missing, and it's a woman to put my arms around. A woman who's smart, caring, considerate, and fucking gorgeous.

I often get beautiful women to go out with me. Hell, sometimes I luck out and find smart with it. But it usually crashes and burns to ash when she's mean to a waiter or insults a child's haircut.

What do I have to do to find a woman that's attractive, kind, and can mentally stimulate me? Sacrifice a goat? A virgin? A virgin goat?

If God, or whoever controls my fate up there, could also see fit to make her like basketball, I'd be eternally grateful.

"Look who it is," a voice tinkles from halfway across the bar. Looking up, I see Samantha Hillis wave and walk straight to us with a smile meant only for Landon. "What are you two handsome men doing here? This is such a coincidence. Isn't this a coincidence, Laney?"

Samantha gestures to the woman who's walked in behind her and obviously trying to hide behind Samantha. Laney really doesn't need to hide from me, though. I've known her for over half her life and have seen her on her worst days. I've seen her when her swimsuit strap broke and she came up from the water without her top. Truth be told, that was one of my favorite memories of Laney Wyatt, but I couldn't stare too hard in front of Landon that day.

I know her nipples are pink, and I know I want to wrap my lips around them like they're gumdrops.

I eye the bucket of beer on the table and silently hope she'll help herself. She deserves it. Landon only convinced me to come out because Laney got fired today. Her eyes are red from crying, and the look on her face does something to my chest. I've never told Landon or shown it, but every time I see Laney sad, my heart feels like it's going to drop out of my butthole.

"Beer?" I ask, nodding at the bucket and trying to meet Laney's eyes.

"I'll go to the bar and order," she says in a soft voice and staring at the floor. I want to put my finger under her chin, tilt her face up to mine, and tell her I'll buy her anything she wants. I know she won't accept my help, though.

And I would help her. I'd at least pay what was left on her student loan for her. If she'd let me help with a down payment on a new car, I'd give it to her. I grip the edge of the table, desperately wanting to help her...with anything.

There was a time when I thought of Laney as something akin to an annoying sibling. I was over at her house so much as a teen that I refer to her mom and dad as my second set of parents. Her dad taught me how to drive a stick shift and play golf. Her mother made me care packages when I was away at college, always sending homemade cookies and rolls of quarters for the old-fashioned washing machines in my dorm basement. I could always count on a package of new socks or new pens and fast-food restaurant gift cards from the Wyatts.

I ate Laney's groceries for almost ten years of my life. It was only around the time I graduated from college that I felt the urge to eat her "groceries." I've spent the last several years looking away from my best friend's sister and trying not to give it away that I'd bend her over a table and eat her from the back at every wedding, funeral, and birthday party we've attended together.

I run my eyes up the length of her. Fit body from long walks I know she takes most mornings. Long, dark hair with deep brown eyes you can get lost in. A small mole on her neck I want to kiss. My mouth waters at the very sight of her lately.

"Do you want me to kick Wayno's ass?" Landon asks, kicking the chair next to him and gesturing for Laney to sit down. Damn. I should have pulled the chair out next to me so I could at least inhale the vanilla scent I've come to associate with her.

Laney flops into the chair and rests her head on the table, her hair flopping into her face. Landon picks up a hunk of hair to look into her eyes, and I wish it was my hand holding that gorgeous long hair. I'd hold it while I ride...

"They said they didn't need as many paralegals now that technology can do some of the drafting and research work," Laney says, pulling me out of thoughts of riding her from behind.

"You'll find something," Landon says.

"Not before my piss-ass week severance runs out. I was already scrimping." Her eyes flick to mine, and I tilt my head, angling my face so we can look at each other directly and willing myself to hold eye contact. Landon can go fuck himself if he reads too much into my expression. "That severance will pay Chantel for the utilities and about half the rent I owe for this month. I applied as a rideshare driver on the way here to hopefully get enough for the rest."

I'm done with this shit. "Why don't you let me help? I'll lend you a month's rent, Laney. No interest. Pay it back when you have it."

Samantha pulls a chair next to Landon and scoots it within six inches of my best friend's body. I swear she'd ride his jock like a mechanical bull if he'd pay her any attention. "Let Milo help you," Samantha says, looking between Laney and Landon like she's watching a tennis match and deciding where she wants to focus her attention. "There's nothing wrong with letting someone help you."

Laney lifts her head and squares her shoulders. Here we go. Here's that Wyatt stubbornness I was expecting. "No way," she says as the waitress comes by with appetizer plates and takes an order from Samantha for something Samantha simply points to on the menu. "I don't want to owe you money, Milo. It would dig me into a hole on top of being in trouble. It's better I just deal with it the best I can."

"You won't owe me for a very long time," I say. Fuck, my fingers itch to touch her hand.

Laney's favorite beer suddenly appears in front of her, and a plate of mozzarella sticks, also her favorite, materializes on the table. She eyes the plate, and her eyes fill with tears again.

This time, I don't stop myself for Landon's sake. Let him read into it what he wants. I put my arm around Laney and scoot her chair closer to me. I grimace a little at the scratching sound the chair makes against the floor. Her shoulders stiffen at my touch. Am I that repulsive to her? "Let us help you, even if it's ordering mozzarella sticks."

Laney looks at her brother. "You didn't have to feed me tonight."

Landon shakes his head. "I didn't. Milo did when we got here."

"I told the waitress to bring mozzarella sticks and a Blue Moon with an orange slice to the beautiful brunette when she sees you."

Laney leans her head on my shoulder, and my dick twitches against my zipper. If only Landon and Samantha would disappear from the table. I could almost close my eyes and pretend I'm on a date with Laney.

She takes a deep breath and blows it out. "I don't suppose you know a paralegal job I could apply to?"

"Funny you should ask," I say. Her head jerks off my shoulder, and she looks at me, blinking twice like I just answered her prayers. I miss her leaning against me so much that I regret ever saying something. "Don't get too excited. It's a maternity leave and doesn't start for about another two weeks. Landon told me what happened, and I gave a heads-up to our human resources that I know someone reputable who just got laid off. It can feed you for a couple months and buy you some time. But I wish you'd let me help with the next couple weeks."

"Maybe the driving app can come through on that?" Samantha suggests. I wish she'd shut up and just let me work it out with Laney how my best friend's little sister can be a kept woman for a couple weeks.

The look of relief on Laney's face almost pushes me to bury my face in her hair and whisper her name over and over, promising to take care of her forever. I've never felt this with another woman, not even my college girlfriend. I want to build a dam of bubble wrap around Laney so nothing can ever hurt her. I want to fuck her like the woman she is now and protect her like the vulnerable little geek with scabby knees I've known her as for years.

"We just need to get you through a few weeks until the paycheck comes," Landon says.

"*If* I get this job." Laney throws her head back and looks at the ceiling. "They could choose someone else."

"If you're interested, I'll make another call. You'll get it."

Fuck, I love being her savior.

"Plan!" Samantha says, clapping her hands. "Milo will get you the temp job, I'll help with your resume and make sure Wayno gives you the reference he promised so you can start looking for a permanent job, and you'll use severance and driving money to pay for stuff until then."

"Uh, one thing," I say, holding up a finger. Laney reaches for a mozzarella stick, and I push the entire plate toward her. They're all hers. "The salary for the temp job may be a little less than what you were making."

She chews a mozzarella stick and licks a drop of sauce off the corner of her mouth. My own tongue licks my bottom lip at the thought of licking that off her skin.

"So, I'll need to keep driving and scrounge for odd jobs anyway. I'm fucked," she says. "I hardly have time to drive people to the airport if I get a temp job. I just need money to rain from the sky."

"You could sell your body," Landon says, and I immediately glare at him. "It's the oldest profession. No shame in it."

"Thanks, bro," Laney says.

"You could sell your dirty underwear," Samantha says, and everyone goes silent.

Laney stares at her friend, mouth open and a funny look on her face like she was just punched. Samantha doesn't notice and simply smiles at the waitress who sets a platter of pretzel bites in front of her.

"Excuse me?" Laney asks. "What did you say about my underwear?"

Samantha picks up a pretzel and dips it into the beer cheese sauce. "Haven't you heard of this? Women sell their dirty panties online, and filthy-minded men that probably live in cabins in Montana or something buy them. I guess there are few sites out there that do this."

Crickets. I scrunch my face in confusion, Landon tilts his head, and Laney freezes with a mozzarella stick halfway to her mouth. "Why?" We all ask it at the same time.

Samantha shrugs. "Do I look like I'm a pervert living in a Montana cabin? I don't know. Do they masturbate with them? Use them to fill holes in the wall so the mice don't get in? Use them to strain moonshine and give it extra flavor? I don't know, but it's a thing."

Heat moves up my neck. Buying a girl's dirty panties to rub off to them?

Hold on – masturbating with Laney Wyatt's dirty panties? I wouldn't be opposed to it, but I *would* be opposed to other men jerking off with her dirty panties.

"Laney wouldn't do that!" I sputter.

"I'm just desperate enough, I'd think about it," she says, sticking another mozzarella stick into her mouth. "How much do the women make?"

"No! Nope. Not happening," Landon says. He scowls, and I notice, for the millionth time, how much he looks like Laney when he's confused or angry. Dark hair. Dark eyes. Same expression when he tilts his head to the side and stares you down. He's the male version of her but a foot taller and without the luscious chest area I want to nibble.

"I'm a grown woman, asshole. If I want to sell my sweaty panties on a website, you can't say anything about it."

Landon reddens and grits his teeth. I shake my head, silently pleading with him to stop challenging Laney. She's always done what she wants to do. The easiest way to ensure Laney will do something is to tell her she can't do it.

Laney stares at the wall across from her as she eats and sips her beer. "Are they silky, or can you just sell the cotton kind from Walmart?"

Samantha chokes on her own beer and wipes her face before answering. "You can't even be considering this? I was just fucking around. It's probably something stupid like clearing a couple bucks. You'd have to ship them and stuff, too."

This is the train of thought I need to latch onto. "Yeah, you'd have shipping costs. Bubble mailers are expensive. Do they even let you charge more for international? Even worse, what if someone local buys them? What if you ship them and it's someone like your old band teacher?"

"They wouldn't know who she is."

Landon and I both widen our eyes, hoping Samantha gets the hint and shuts the fuck up.

"But Laney would know," Landon says.

Laney shakes her head like she's waking up from a long sleep and blinks. "It's a stupid idea. I'll stick with rideshare and apply to one of those shopping apps. It'll be enough to pay the bills, but I may have to talk to the hospital about the medical bill or something. I sure wouldn't want old Mr. Hagerfeld from band to order my underwear. What if I ran into him at the post office?" She shakes her head in frustration and takes a long drink of beer. She sets it down when she's done and sucks on the orange slice from the rim of her glass. "It's a joke. Who even does that?"

Profiled

LANEY

My hands shake as my fingers hover over the keyboard. "What should I put for my pubic hair?" I ask Chantel.

My roommate walks over to my laptop and squints at the screen. She blows on the cup of coffee she's holding and pulls at the belt of her long, gray cardigan as she examines the choice bubbles. "That's a question? They really want to know how you groom the old beaver?"

"I don't know what to do." I point at the screen and lean back in my chair, blowing out a frustrated sigh. "This entire thing is fucking crazy. I have to fill out a section about myself, and I have no idea what to write. I thought I'd start with demographics and come back to the profile. This is scary. I've never told strangers about my shaving routine."

How it got to this, I'll never know. I've been driving people to the airport or picking them up when their car breaks down for the last week, but I've heard nothing from the food delivery app. They must have enough people for now. Milo came through on the temp job interview, but that's not soon enough. By the time I interview and start, I'll be behind on bills and trying to play catchup on less than I was making before.

Samantha's idea about selling my underwear wouldn't leave my head.

Chantel rolls an old desk chair to the table and sets her coffee down. She smooths her dark, medium-length hair with carefully styled waves and smiles, showing her professionally whitened teeth. She cracks her knuckles and blows on her fingertips. "Allow me. This will be fun. Let's see…" Her voice trails off as she studies the website. "Country? That's easy enough."

"Afghanistan!" I yell at the same time she mumbles, "United States."

She looks at me and smirks. "Afghanistan?"

"It's the first country, other than the one I live in, that I thought of. I don't want this associated with me in any way."

"Afghanistan was the first country you thought of? Not Canada? Not – I don't know – Belgium? You won't get any buyers anyway. The guys have to pay shipping. They aren't going to want to pay for shipping from Afghanistan. Use your brain."

"That's just stereotyping, Chantel. I'm shocked at you. There are plenty of buyers that may live in Afghanistan."

"You're selling your underwear to make money, but you'll sell it to men in Afghanistan and charge them local shipping when you're really shipping from the other side of the world?"

I blow out a breath. "Fine. Put my real country. But if I'm easily found and brutally murdered by my panty stalker, you'll feel bad."

She gives me a side-eyed look but doesn't argue with me further. "What's your username?"

We both sit in silence for a moment. I take a bite of the ramen noodles beside me and look at the sad bowl. I can do this. I have to do this. I like ramen noodles, but I'm going to eat them for every meal if I don't get some cash. "I didn't get that far. Ideas?"

Chantel takes over my mousepad and drives, navigating around the site to the "sellers" link. "What are other sellers using?"

I shrug. "It looks like a combination of their names with numbers behind them or naming themselves after food. This one is called Lemonade4321421." I point at the screen. "See what I mean?"

"Do you think she pees in them? Get it? Lemonade?"

"Fucking gross."

Chantel curls into a laugh, and her hair flops into her face. I eye her coffee cup, hoping she doesn't spill it on my keyboard. I sure as fuck can't afford a new laptop.

"Maybe her panties ta-taste s-sour," she says, laughing so hard she can hardly get the words out. She slaps the desk next to her, sending a pen rolling to the floor.

"I don't know why I asked you for help. You're utterly useless."

She straightens, laughing quietly, and resumes scrolling through the other sellers. Her shoulders still shake with laughter as she tries to pull her shit together. "There are a lot of users named after candy. We could do that."

"I feel like that's lying to the buyer. Do they expect my panties to taste like licorice if I use that as a username?" I ask, pulling the collar of my sweatshirt over my face. I could hide in this fabric and just die that this is what my life has become.

Chantel sniffs. "OK, let's think about this. Guys, and maybe some girls that buy used underwear, are buying used panties because they want them filthy, right? Some of the big sellers here advertise that they're wet and stuff. Maybe we give you a username that implies they're really dirty?"

"Dirtypanties123?"

She waffles her head from side to side. "That doesn't stand out enough. We know they're dirty. That's why you're selling them on this site. We need to dig deep here...like you're pulling a thong out of your butt crack kind of deep."

I take a swipe at her but she dodges my slap and points to her drink. "I'm so fucking glad that you find this funny," I say. "Your roommate is selling her soiled panties on the Internet to pay your ass rent, and you have all the jokes. Thanks so much for your support."

Chantel straightens up, sober as a nun. "That's it."

"What's it?" I ask.

"You said, 'soiled.' That's your schtick."

"Soiled?"

Chantel bites her lip and stares at my screen with the website logo on it. "HeavilySoiled. One word. You don't need it to be two. It gives you an air of importance. Like Cher."

"I'm done with life."

"Hear me out! They're here for dirty underwear. From the looks of it, the girl with the dirtiest panties wins, right? If they see your username, they'll know they're getting a real piece of work."

"That would mean I would have to...heavily soil them."

"Is that a problem?"

I stare at my roommate like I've never seen her before. "Are you high?"

She waves her arm at the nearby window. "Sit outside in sweatpants on a hot day. Eat four questionable burritos and then go for a run. This is the kind of shit these kinky bastards live for. Fart! Don't cross your legs when you sneeze! Let the river run, Laney. Rejoice in your weak bladder."

"Do not type that," I say, trying to pry her hand away from the mouse. Unfortunately, she clicks the letters in the username area, and a screen congratulating me on having an unused username comes up.

"I'm going to put a pillow over your face tonight while you sleep!"

"Too late, HeavilySoiled. Let's talk about who you are as a person, shall we?"

I pull my head back into my sweatshirt and pull the drawstrings. "Doesn't matter. Type whatever you think will sell. You will anyway. I can't believe I let you help me with this."

"You asked me for help so you could actually sell some shit. Now, where were we?" She flips through a couple of pages in the profile section. "Pubic hair trim?"

"Shaved," I mumble from inside my sweatshirt.

"That's not a choice."

"What are the options?"

"Let's see. Would you classify your pubic hair situation as a full bush, postage stamp, silver fox, landing strip, baby's butt smooth, or glitter?"

"Glitter?"

She smiles and turns back to the screen. "I don't want glitter all over the apartment. You can't vacuum that up."

"Fair enough. Baby's butt smooth."

Chantel makes a sucking sound with her mouth. "Let's go with full bush."

"What?" I ask, peeking out from the shirt again to stare open-mouthed at the screen. "I hate pubic hair."

"These people are kinky, Laney. They like dirty panties. Think like them for one fucking minute," she says, tapping her temple. "They want filthy. You'll sweat more with full pubic hair. They'll cling to the hope that a stray, curly strand will be stuck in the fabric."

I let her type without trying to stop her. "Boobs?" she asks.

"Yes," I say. "I have them."

"Huge," she mumbles, typing again.

"I have a B cup that pushes into a C cup in PMS and excess salt consumption. I hardly think anyone is going to believe I'm huge."

"Are you going to post pictures of your boobs?"

"What? No!"

Chantel shrugs. "Then what are you worried about?" She turns and smiles at me again. "It's not like the men of Afghanistan are going to see your titties, so what's the big deal? It's all about the mental picture these men will form of you in their minds."

I lean back in my chair and let Chantel take complete control of the situation. "Sexual orientation?" She shimmies her shoulders. "Obviously bisexual."

"Why bisexual?"

"If women are on here looking for dirty panties, it gives them hope."

"Why don't they wear their own panties and play with those?"

Chantel furrows her brow like I stumped her on that one. "Uh, different flavors? They may want to try some new beef."

I shrug. Personally, I'm more offended about the big bush than Chantel lying and saying that I'm bisexual.

Chantel types for several minutes, and I can't bear to look at the screen. I eat in silence as she hums to herself and looks out the window like she's not really seeing whatever is out there. She chews on the inside of her cheek like she does when she's doing something that requires complete concentration.

Eventually, she leans back and gives the air a chef's kiss. "Perfection."

"Do I want to know what you wrote for my profile?"

She waves me forward and I emotionally brace myself for what I'm about to see.

About me: "I'm a postal worker, so I'm on the move all day every day. I sweat. I fart because I have stomach issues when I eat raw vegetables. I pee a little when I laugh or sneeze hard. If you buy my underwear, I can guarantee they've been put through the paces. I'm no delicate flower.

I'll wear thongs, bikinis, or boy shorts and will take requests if the price is right. I mostly wear cotton because silk or lace isn't comfortable on my plump vulva, but you'll see a few of those.

Let's negotiate."

A small groan comes from my throat. "I want to circle back to that me killing you in your sleep thing," I say as Chantel slaps the desk again, doubled over laughing. "Why am I a postal worker?"

"I needed something where you'd have really gross underwear. You need a job where you move all day."

"A nurse? A construction worker? You didn't think of these? You went straight for a federal worker."

"It was the first thing that came to mind."

"Why is my vulva plump? Is that even a thing to aspire to? Is there a thirty minute workout that will plump up a vulva?"

Chantel shrugs. "I thought it would be a selling point! Think of it like the word *engorged* in romance novels."

"You have to be fucking kidding me."

"There's probably some man out there thinking to himself how much he wants to find a woman with a plump vulva and full pubic hair."

I smile sarcastically. "Don't forget my ginormous titties."

Chantel snaps her fingers and points at me, smiling. "Now you're thinking like the saleslady I know you can be." She turns back to the screen. "Do you have the panties? We could load pictures." She scrolls through a few seller pages, clucking as she goes. This is obviously entertainment to her. "It looks like you can load the pictures and entice people to buy them before you wear them and get them nasty. At least, that's one way to do it. One woman here wears them first and then shows the crotch."

"What if they have skid marks?"

Chantel sputters a drink of her coffee into her cup. "I feel like that's something you could charge double for on this site."

Ignoring her, I reach into the bag at my feet and pull out the panties I got from the clearance bin at Bucky's Bargain House. There are no frills with them. Most are cotton. A few are black and lacy. The cotton pairs were three for five bucks. The lacy black numbers were three bucks each. If I sell them for twenty-five bucks – which seems to be the average going price – I'll more than make the cost of the underwear back. Buyers also pay for shipping, and I bought cheap sandwich bags and yellow mailer envelopes that would only run about a buck per pair cost for me. If my calculations are correct, I should clear around twenty smackers on the most expensive underwear. If I can sell a few pairs a week, I can cover the gas bill and a cart of food every couple weeks.

I really have no idea what to expect as far as moving product, though.

Chantel and I work at positioning the underwear in different ways on the floor. Folded in one picture. Flat in the next. Some women model the underwear, complete with a photo of a slit wedgie, but there is never going to be a day when I take a picture of my pussy area to model used underwear. The buyers will have to purchase based on pictures of the underwear on my uninteresting beige carpet.

We take a few pictures in silence, and Chantel sends the shots to my email. When she turns back to my laptop, she quietly loads the pictures, marks them for easy organization to keep track of inventory, makes a complete spreadsheet for me to record sales, shipping dates, and tracking numbers, and posts the pictures to the seller page.

I blink twice as I watch my pictures populate my seller account. Chantel nods and smiles. "They're out in the world. We just wait and see now." She turns to look at me. If I'm half as green as I feel, it's no wonder her face wrinkles in concern. "It's fine, Laney."

"Fine is not a word I would use to describe any of this." I nudge her aside. "Now that this is done, I need to look for a real job."

Chantel moves out of the chair, taking her now-empty coffee cup as she goes. "We can load your socks later."

I spin around in the chair so fast that it swivels all the way in a circle. When I get it right, I stare open-mouthed. "Socks?"

"Yeah, they sell used socks in addition to panties."

"Why would anyone want to buy used socks?"

"Foot fetishes are huge, Laney. How sheltered are you? Besides, selling your dirty socks isn't as bad as selling panties, right?"

"I can't imagine I'll make a lot from selling dirty socks."

"The first model on a cam site probably said something similar. You never know how deranged an average member of the American public is, sweetheart. Personally, I think you should sell everything you can on this site. Do they allow bras?"

"I'm so worried someone will find out. What if someone's wearing my socks, and notices they look like a pair I was wearing a week ago?"

"You're worried someone in our small town will find out that another member of the community bought your dirty socks?"

I nod and bite at a cuticle on my left hand. "Yes."

Chantel walks to me and bends down to pat my leg. "Of all the states in the United States and of all the cities in those states, I don't think anyone down at the gas station will notice that someone is wearing your socks that you sold on a panty-selling site. You're completely anonymous. Just buy generic, white socks if you're worried about it. Nobody said you have to monogram them."

She raises her eyebrows and smiles. "I know about this. Samantha knows because she gave you the idea. Not one other soul will ever find out," she says. "Let's take your mind off this. Landon is having people over tonight. Let's go. I even have a bottle of wine you can pass off as your own party host gift."

Eavesdropping

MILO

"Do you want another glass of wine?" I ask, shaking the bottle of Riesling in front of Laney.

She looks so beautiful tonight. I only agreed to have a few people over when Landon suggested a small party because I was hoping she'd come. She showed up with tight, black leggings that leave little to the imagination and a long, blue sweater that hangs off her right shoulder, showing the black tank top and her white bra strap I long to reach out and run my finger down. Black boots are tied at her ankles. Her hair is down, and I itch to wind my fingers through it.

She shakes her head. "No thanks, Milo. I think I'll just head out."

No. She can't leave. I haven't made her fall in love with me yet, which is what I want to do every time I'm around her. I want to sweep her into my arms and run away. Maybe go for a horseback ride on a beach somewhere, with her hair blowing against my face as I sit behind her. "You haven't stayed long. Chantel's still going strong. Can I drive you home?"

She cocks her head and smirks at me. "You've been drinking all night, Milo, and I brought my car. I've only had one glass, and that was an hour ago. I think I'll be fine."

Damn. I really wanted to take her home. I could drive to her house and tuck her into bed while her brother stayed here, out of sight and out of mind. I watch sadly as she picks up her peacoat. I watch her put her gloves on finger by finger, button every single button on the coat, and make sure she pulls the beanie hat with the pom pom on it all the way down to cover her ears. They shouldn't be cold. Nothing on her should ever be cold, in pain, or ever inconvenienced.

I open the door for her and smile. "Have a good night, Laney," I say, pulling her in for a friendly hug. It's the same hug I've been using on her the better part of a decade. She probably thinks it's a friendly hug between people who have known each other for years. What she doesn't know is that my balls feel as full as water balloons every time we do it. "Catch you later."

She walks out the door, and I wait on the top step of our small porch. She turns and waves again. "Are you going to watch me walk to the car?"

"Sure fucking am."

"Whatever, Milo. Thanks for making sure I'm safe, I guess."

Yep. Making sure she's safe. Watching her ass move as she walks away. Same thing.

As soon as she's in her car, buckled, and pulling away, I shut the door and grab the bottle of wine I left on our entryway table. Blowing out a sigh, I look around for other people I want to talk to. A few people that Landon works with linger in the living room, but they're consumed in their own work conversation. Some women that Landon has tried setting me up with are holed up next to the avocado dip in the kitchen, so that's out. Eventually, I head to the basement door and reach for the light switch.

Huh? It's already on. That's weird. Is someone down here doing the stereotypical make-out session in the basement? I creep down the stairs, still holding the bottle of wine. I raise it to my lips as I walk, ready to look around the corner and catch a couple mid fuck.

I freeze halfway down the steps, the bottle of wine still raised. "HeavilySoiled is the username we chose. Well, I chose it," someone says. Is that Chantel?

"One word or two?" another voice asks in a whisper.

"One. Like Cher."

"For fuck's sake. I wish she'd just let us help her. Should we crowd-fund her medical bills? It would take something off her plate," the other voice says, a little louder this time. It takes me a moment to recognize the voice as Samantha's. "I feel so awful. I almost slipped Wayno a laxative in his coffee today. Fucker. I just can't believe she's actually going through with it. I mean, talk about icky."

Through with what?

I flatten myself against the wall and hold as still as possible. I'm even mindful of my breathing. They're obviously talking about Laney, and maybe they snuck down here to have a private conversation about her. Are they being catty? Should I call them out on it? How dare they talk shit about my goddess of everything I know about attraction?

"I'll pay the water bill outright this month for her. I'm not going to accept money for it," Chantel says. "If she insists on paying me back, she can do that after she gets a job. I hope the driving thing picks up. It's not as busy this time of year in Minnesota. No baseball and cold as snot."

Samantha hums and says something I can't hear. It sounds like this is more of a conversation about helping Laney than it is talking shit about her. It warms my heart that Laney has such wonderful friends.

"Think Milo will come through on the temp job?" Samantha asks. "She desperately needs something stable."

"Laney trusts him. Then again, Laney trusts everyone. But Hot Coulson should come through."

Hot Coulson? I can't help but smirk and bite my lip. They think I'm hot.

Hold on. Does Laney also think I'm hot? Do the women ever talk about me over brunch and wonder what I'm like in bed? Does Laney call me Hot Coulson? Because I'd very much like that.

"Well, maybe she won't have to sell her panties for long."

Stop the fucking bus. All fantasies of Laney guessing my dick size to Samantha and Chantel over mimosas stop suddenly. Like a record scratching at a DJ'd event.

What the actual fuck?

"If she sells any at all. I mean, there can't be that many men out there who are willing to buy a gal's dirty underwear. The site seemed oversaturated when I scrolled through it. I wouldn't say anything to Laney about that, though. We should be supportive and think of ways to make money."

"She's really doing this?" Samantha asks.

"Some of the pictures are nasty – full-on snatch shots and pics of soaking wet panties no bigger than dental floss that are shoved so far up a slit you can hardly see them. You know Laney. She had her panties neatly laid out to position them because she'd never model them on that site. Never in a million years. I can't believe I actually got her to accept the name HeavilySoiled."

My eyebrows practically shoot up to my hairline. Are Laney's panties heavily soiled, or is it a gimmick? It has to be total bullshit. She doesn't seem the poor hygiene type. Then again, my dick twitches at the thought of Laney's panties being utterly filthy. Wet. Maybe a little dirty just so they smell nice and...used.

"My nephew needs a babysitter a few nights a month. My brother and his wife pay well. Do you think Laney would be willing to do that?" Samantha asks, her voice receding as I silently slink back up the stairs.

I quietly open the door and quickly shut it behind me, hoping Samantha and Chantel don't hear it and wonder if someone is coming or going from the basement. I quickly lean over the kitchen counter and grab a handful of chips as the door opens.

The girls come into the kitchen and look left and right, frowning. "Milo, did someone come up from the basement just now?" Chantel asks.

Damn. They heard the door. I paste an innocent look on my face and shake my head as I dip a chip into guacamole. "I don't think so."

"We thought we heard the door while we were having a private conversation."

I shrug. "There was a group of people just standing over there. They could have bumped it." I chew my chips like there's nothing to see here and I don't know the girl I've been in lust with for years has gone rogue and is selling her panties for everyone to buy.

Everyone to buy.

Everyone includes me, right?

I look away and dip another chip. "Were you girls really making out with each other down there? Come on. You can tell Daddy Milo," I say with a wink.

Samantha crosses her arms and laughs. "You're sick, Milo."

She has no idea how sick I am and the disturbing stuff I'm going to order online as soon as I can get up to my room without drawing attention to my absence.

***

"HeavilySoiled. HeavilySoiled. One word. Where are you, darling?" I ask under my breath, tapping keys on my laptop and grimacing at some of the panties and pictures on the websites I search. Lord, this is a rabbit hole of depravity I wasn't expecting to go down. Chantel was right about the pictures on these websites.

Mixed emotions run through my mind. I hate that other men may have already ordered her underwear and are wrapping it around their fists or sniffing it as we speak. My fingers shake with jealous rage as I scroll. The other emotions are desperation and curiosity. What does Laney's underwear look like? I also *have* to buy a pair before I get ready for bed. I won't be able to sleep tonight unless I have one shipped to me. Knowing that obtaining a pair of her panties is an option has me shaken to my core.

A picture of a black lace pair of panties populates my screen under the username HeavilySoiled on the third site I check, and I breathe a sigh of relief. There's at least one pair that hasn't been sold to an incel in his mother's basement.

I look at the description and tilt my head in confusion. Full bush? Huh. I would have thought she'd keep it trim. At least, that's what I imagined when I jerked off to her.

Wait. Huge boobs?

I look back at the username. Yep. That's the one I overheard Samantha and Chantel talking about. Did she lie about her boob size? Did she also lie about her lack of trim skills?

I scroll further and find a detailed personal introduction that is not Laney. She's never worked for the postal service. I really don't want to buy a random woman's underwear, but it's not like I can text Laney and say something like, "Oh, hey. I was casually looking around a dirty panty site and wondered if this HeavilySoiled person is you. I'm buying a pair. Let me know!"

Christ, I'd rather die.

I read the description again and think. This reeks of Chantel's sense of humor. Did she write it? Maybe Laney was so embarrassed or couldn't think of anything good to write. Looking back at the picture of the black panties, they look like Laney's taste. Simple. Classic. They look like something a stereotypical girl next door would wear. The kind of underwear the woman you'd take home to meet your mother would buy for a weekend trip. They're also around what I would imagine her size to be.

I blow out a breath, thinking. If I was selling my underwear on the Internet and wanted to remain anonymous, I would make shit up. This has to be the case. Unless Samantha and Chantel have gone out of the way to prank me by luring me to buy panties on the Internet, it has to be Laney. They looked pretty worried when they thought they'd been overheard in the basement, so a prank is out of the question unless they're up for best acting awards.

My cursor hovers over the purchase option. There's no going back from this. I don't have to buy more than one pair. I'll just have one sent to me, see what they smell like, maybe lick them once just to ease my curiosity, and never go to this site again. The idea of gorgeous

Laney sitting sweetly on her floor and carefully packaging this pair of underwear just for my use does things to my chest.

I squeeze my eyes shut, cringe, and click the purchase button. A weird gurgling sound comes from my throat as the site moves me to the next page in the purchase process – like I've been accepted into the panty buying club. In fact, as I go to the next page, I can either checkout as a member or a guest. "Definitely guest," I say to myself. "I wonder if they have a punch card or something."

Question answered. As I go to yet another page, the system asks if I'm sure I don't want to join because I get a free pair of panties if I buy ten.

I think for a moment, tapping my thumbs on the laptop mouse. Will I buy that much of Laney's underwear, enough to make an eleventh worth it?

I'll worry about that later. For now, I need to focus on this single pair of black panties. I can come back if I want more.

The next screen is the shipping screen.

Fuuuuuuuucccccccckkkkkk. I cannot put in my shipping information. I didn't think this through. What did I think would happen? A briefcase drop at a park? A drone delivery to a secret warehouse? If the shipping address matches the same address as her brother, she'll either think her brother's a freak, or she'll know it's me. This can't happen, even though I'd be more than happy to blame Landon.

I run my hands through my hair and ponder a way around this. There has to be a way around this. I stare out my window and look at the moon hovering over the park landscape across the street. As I think, a dog barks from next door, and sounds of Landon's party guests leaving fill the night under my window.

I could open a post office box, I guess. That's it. I'll drive over to Wisconsin after work tomorrow and open a rural post office box. She won't think anything about sending something over the border to Wisconsin. I'll go further up I-94 so it won't raise eyebrows, but it won't be too far of a drive for me.

This could work.

I open another tab and Google post office boxes in Wisconsin. The post office link comes up first on the screen, but I don't click it because I'm too busy looking at the sponsored link under it.

What the fuck is a virtual mailbox?

I click on the link, hoping I'm not going to be taken to a spam site, and the heavens open. Virtual mailboxes can collect your mail for you, scan it, and even forward it to you to your real address if you request it. This sounds shady as fuck, but it's a real thing. Wow. Talk about workarounds for illegal activity in a certain state.

I scroll further through the information and do a few more Google searches that verify that these things are real. Apparently, they specifically cater to American citizens who live abroad and need an American address for mail. There's even one in a legitimate shipping store across the border in Wisconsin. Bingo. I should get one somewhat close in case there's a problem with getting the package to me and I have to drive over. I don't trust these things yet.

I spend a few minutes filling out the information, scan my ID while crossing my fingers this isn't just a great scam to get identity information, and I have a virtual mailbox in fifteen minutes. When it's ready, I head back to the panty site and fill in my new shipping address, giggling to myself the entire time.

Holy fucking shit, I'm totally going to get a pair of Laney's panties sent directly to my house from my virtual service, and she'll never be any wiser.

Panty Rich

LANEY

"How was your day?" Chantel asks, stomping snow from her boots on the welcome mat and dropping her keys on the counter.

"A toddler threw up in my backseat, and the mother only tipped me four dollars. I spent five cleaning the car at the car wash. My other ride tipped worse. All my tips go to gas money to work the actual job. How was your day?"

"Not as exciting as having a toddler puke in my car. Did you look for jobs?"

"Yeah, I have a first-round interview with a divorce attorney's law office in Stansburg," I say, referencing a town on the other side of the county. I'm not looking forward to that commute. "Cross your fingers, though. It's good money. Milo's company also reached out and offered me about enough to cover rent. It'll be eight weeks of maternity leave. I start next Monday," I say with a sigh. "At least that's something."

"Did you check your underwear account?"

I toss my head back and grunt. "Not yet. And can we stop calling it that?" I ask. "I'm scared. What if nobody wants my underwear? I mean, how embarrassing is that? Am I so disgusting that a man doesn't want my used panties?"

"I think disgusting is the entire point." Chantel hangs up her coat and sits next to me on our brown sofa. "Is that the only thing you're worried about?"

"No," I say, fiddling with a thread on the blue throw pillow on my lap. "I'm also worried someone *did* buy my underwear."

"Can't have it both ways."

"This entire thing is fucking crazy."

Chantel leans forward and grabs my laptop from the bottom of the coffee table shelf where I store it. She puts it gently on my lap and opens the screen. "Log in," she demands.

"No."

"Log in, or I'll break into your email somehow and log you in myself."

"That's rude," I say, crossing my arms. "Probably illegal, too."

"Rude? Rude is buying bargain underwear, creating a seller account to sell them, and never letting your roommate know how much money you're making. Come on, Lancy. I have a vested interest here. I have a landlord to pay." Her eyes widen like she's just had an evil idea. She rubs her hands together and bites her lip. "I could tell Mr. Borris that our rent is late because you haven't checked your dirty panty site."

"You wouldn't."

"What in our entire relationship indicates I wouldn't go that far?"

She's right. Chantel would sing like a canary to our landlord if she thought she could get out of paying. Even worse, Mr. Borris would probably try to find my panties on a seller website.

I give Chantel one last dirty look and type the login information, grimacing as I enter the username. I can't believe I let her give me that name. It'll haunt me forever.

As the screen loads, I grip the couch cushion under me. I can handle it if someone doesn't buy my underwear. Plenty of women on the page model the underwear they're selling, and I won't go that far. It won't be a surprise when I don't sell anything. I'll take it in stride. It's not a personal knock against me since my picture isn't on the site. It's probably why I didn't sell my products.

Except I did sell something.

I sold a lot of things.

My eyes bug out of my head when I see the amount of money in my account. There's $148.45 in the account, and It's ready to be transferred to my bank account with one click. Before it disappears, I quickly tap the button to request a transfer. This is too good to be true, and I don't want my money taken away over a clerical error. "Chantel, holy shit. Come here!"

"Did you sell a pair?" she asks, sitting on the couch next to me and looking over my shoulder.

"No! I sold six."

Chantel lets out a low whistle. "Damn. Maybe I should sell my underwear for that trip I've been wanting. Shit, Laney. After fees, you made almost $150 with the included shipping. With shipping something so light and the panties being so cheap, you'll easily clear $120." She reaches for my mouse and scrolls down the shipping page for me. "Where did they order from?"

"None from Afghanistan."

She slowly turns toward me, squinting. "Lucky break."

"Look," I say, pointing to the page. My finger shakes as I touch the screen and scroll down further. "A guy in Idaho bought three. He's obviously a total freak. One guy is in Louisiana, and another guy is in North Carolina. The closest person is in Wisconsin." My shoulders slouch, and I blow out a breath. "That's a relief that it's not my old band teacher."

"And you were worried you wouldn't sell any. Laney, this could really help until you get going with Milo's company and driving picks up in the spring. This just paid your half of the gas bill and your half of the trash and sewer bills. Sell a few more, and you'll be able to buy a cart of groceries. If you do this regularly, you can pay your school loan every month."

I look at the screen again and do some quick math. Actually, if I sell double what I did this week, I could pay off what's left on the school loan in a few months, never to worry about it again.

Relief washes over me, but I shouldn't be so calm. I now have to package my dirty underwear when I take it off every night. I know my clean freak ways, and I'll itch to wash it before I send it. That would get me a bad rating and would keep customers from being repeat buyers, though. Will I get regular customer if they like my...brand? Talk about pressure. This is the first time my job performance depends on a stranger's sense of smell preferring my special sauce to another seller's.

How did my career concerns morph from doing proper research for a case to making sure my butt is dirty enough for a customer's taste?

I shake my head and grab my laptop. "Where are you going?" Chantel asks.

"I put all the dirty underwear I've been wearing this week in an old, reusable produce bag in my room. I'm going to sort it by what they bought and package it." I stop and smile an evil grin. "What? You're too good to help with this part? Don't want to touch my dirty underthings and watch me put it into shipping envelopes?"

"I draw the line at that," Chantel says, already heading to the cabinet for a wine glass.

"A hundred and fifty bucks," I mutter to myself as I take the stairs up to my room. My heart pounds, and my palms sweat. I haven't been this happy about a little money in my bank account for a long time. My weekly severance just ran out, and this was the breath of fresh air I needed.

I carefully find the produce bag under my bed and dump the dirty underwear into a pile on my carpet. I then grab a marker off my desk along with the packaging supplies I bought.

I scroll down to the first name. Lloyd Biggins. I grimace a little. He sounds old. The idea of sending my underwear to a man with gray chest hair sticking out of a dirty tank top in every direction comes to mind. Is he spitting in his tobacco spittoon right now?

I take a breath and blow it out my nose. "It doesn't matter, Laney," I say to myself. "He's a paying customer and just paid your part of the gas bill."

I place the three pairs of panties he bought into three separate sandwich bags and then rethink it. I can save supplies by just putting them in one sandwich bag. Am I worried about cross contamination or something? It's not a COVID mask, for fuck's sake. Who cares if they touch?

I stick the sandwich bag in the envelope and quickly write the man's name and shipping address on the form.

Return address? Oh shit. The post office didn't let me ship something without one once. What do I put? I really don't want Lloyd Biggins to know where I live. Where can I send this thing if there's a postal error? Think, Laney. Who should get my dirty underwear? Who deserves an anonymous package of smelly panties?

My brain lights up like a lightbulb, and I quickly Google Wayno's address and write it in the top left corner. Take that, bad boss of the year. Sure, his wife may open the package and find a woman's dirty underwear, but karma's a bitch.

I pull the next client's underwear to me. Plain red cotton. This guy in Louisiana left a note that he'd like me to wear them during my period. Sure, bro. Not happening. Hopefully, the red will be enough for him to *think* they're period underwear. Guys don't know any better.

I package those quickly and also package a blue and white polka-dot pair to be shipped to North Carolina. Surprisingly, both of those customers have names that sound like they're from my generation. Blake and Taylor.

I pull out the last pair of panties to be shipped and stare at the black, lacy panties with a bow on the waistband. These were the most comfortable, and I wore them to take Samantha's dog to the dog park one afternoon when it was unseasonably warm. We also went for a run when we were out. They should be good and janky for...

I find his name and squint. Billy Shitner? That's an unfortunate name. I can only imagine the nicknames in middle school. I can't imagine a man with the last name of Shitner is catching a lot of pussy. I fold the panties neatly, place them in the sandwich bag, and slide them into the yellow mailer. I carefully write the mailbox address.

Huh. We go through that town on the way to the Cheese Palace. It's not too far from here. I mean, it's far enough that I don't know anyone there, but now that I know it's within an hour's drive, my heart speeds up a little. Do they ever come over this way?

"Get real, Laney," I mumble under my breath.

When did I start talking to myself? Is this what selling my dirty underwear has done to me? Making me paranoid? It's just a coincidence.

So what if someone who lives within an hour from me happened to buy my panties. If they go looking for me, they'll knock on Wayno's door and ask for HeavilySoiled.

I shouldn't be upset about any of this. I'm paying my bills. I always have a job. I work a job on the side and help people get to the airport. Who cares if I sell my panties for a few weeks if it helps me pay the bills to be a functional member of society? I can pay Chantel for rent and utilities and maybe, just maybe, get my life together and get ahead. There are worse things to do. I don't rob banks, and I've never killed anyone.

I may do this longer than a few weeks. If I do it for months, could I put a down payment on a car that won't eat maintenance costs? Pay off the school loan and pay the medical bill early?

A smile creases my face. Sure, I'll have to move past my mental image of Lloyd Biggins rubbing my panties on his old dick, but we all have jobs we hate.

This will work. I know it will.

Disgracing Polyester

MILO

The packaging isn't anything to write home about. I don't know what I expected, though. Frilly bows with glitter? A box wrapped in birthday paper?

The yellow bubble-wrap mailer is the same type of packaging my credit card company used to rush my new card to me when I was mugged on vacation. Then again, all users of the website are responsible for their own shipping. Sure, I expected more from a woman who scrapbooks and pays meticulous attention to party decorations, but she sent this to me herself. There's no large corporation with branded boxes handling shipping for her. There's no middleman. Laney took her dirty panties off, placed them in a shipping container, and drove to the post office.

Just for me.

Taking a deep breath, I pull on the envelope flap. When it comes away from the base of the mailer, I inhale deeply, expecting to smell her panties as soon as I open it. I want an earthy scent to hit me in the face. Maybe a little sweat. Butterscotch? Peppermint? Brownies? Dear God, I'm finally going to answer the question of what her pussy smells like. When I don't smell anything but the paper smell of the envelope, I look in the package to find a pair of black panties wrapped in a sandwich bag.

Only the best when freshness matters, I guess.

"I'm criminally dirty," I mumble to the panties like they're listening, reaching into the envelope and removing the sandwich bag. "You are a one-way ticket to the gates of hell, but let's see what you look like up close, you beautiful bitches."

I thumb the lace through the plastic bag. There's a small bow on the front of her panties, and they're neatly folded into a triangle like Laney works at a lingerie store and folds underthings for a living. They don't even look worn. I don't want to throw away the envelope. Even the writing on it is special with my fake name and post office box address written in her handwriting – the same handwriting I used to see on her high school notebooks. I can't bear to part with it, so I shove the mailer into my desk drawer, covering it with a small box of envelopes and an unopened bag of ballpoint pens.

Taking my stairs two at a time, I hustle to my bedroom. I can't let Landon see me with his sister's panties. Not that he'd know they were hers. Dear God, I hope not anyway. That would be weird. I just don't want him to come home and see me holding *any* woman's panties in a plastic bag.

I need to go somewhere private. Somewhere I can look at these and appreciate them for the greatness they are.

How am I, a man with a great job and a kick-ass body that pulls any girl I want on an average night out, losing my mind over a pair of my best friend's little sister's panties?

I actually know the answer to that in the dark recesses of my mind. She's always been off-limits. It's tawdry. Forbidden. I've never been allowed to want her in the real world, but I can have her dirty panties on my cock in the confines of my own lair.

I shut my door and quickly move to the window, looking left and right to make sure there are no curious neighbors peeking in. Pulling the blinds down, I chuckle to myself that I even considered that a pervert would be looking into my window in the middle of the day in the hopes of catching me with Laney Wyatt's panties.

I pull apart the plastic bag and hold my breath. Moment of truth. What do these bad boys smell like? I laugh to myself and the sheer ridiculousness of this, but the train has left the station. My whole obsession with that woman is out of control. I grip Laney's panties, bite my lip, and push the fabric against my face, closing my eyes as soon as the smell hits my nose.

They smell...natural. It's the smell of a woman who wore these to the gym. I know she doesn't have a gym membership, but I still like to imagine her running on a treadmill. When I close my eyes, I can practically see the fabric in her ass crack as she runs or lifts. In my fantasy, she'd reach around and pull them out of her butt with a snapping sound.

Maple syrup. That's what she smells like. The mystery that has perplexed me for years is finally solved. The scent makes me imagine pancakes or waffles on Saturday mornings with me making her breakfast and her wearing my shirt and maybe a pair of my boxer briefs.

I plop onto my bed, adjust the pillows behind my head, and slide her panties over my face. If someone came in right now, I'd be fired from my job, kicked out of my home, disowned by my poor mother, and possibly deported. Laney Wyatt's gusset runs all the way from my chin to the bridge of my nose as I loop the leg holes over my ears and cross my arms.

Just breathe.

That's all I do for minutes – breathe her scent. Inhale. Exhale. I close my eyes and think how much I want this scent on my face for real. I'm not surprised when my hand moves to my fly as I imagine Laney sitting on my face and rocking her clit against my tongue.

Unbuckling my belt and unzipping my jeans, I reach my hand inside my pants and bring my already hard dick out of my boxer briefs. "Fuck, Laney," I whisper, smearing precum over my dick for some lube and fisting my cock at the base. "Let me lick that pink pussy until it's red and throbbing for me."

As I jerk myself, I stick my tongue out, licking the crotch of her panties and tasting the fabric. The postmark on the package said Friday. It's Tuesday, and the taste of her is almost gone, but there's a whisper of something. It's sweet but savory at the same time.

Dear fucking Christ, I'm going to come from the taste of her panties because they taste like pie. More specifically, it's the kind of pie that's sweet, addictive, and has the kind of savory undertone that you can half-ass write off as a vegetable.

Laney Wyatt smells like maple syrup and tastes like pumpkin pie.

I'm going to die from the simple pleasure of the smell and taste of her used underwear. They're going to find me right here with her panties still covering my dead face, my dick in my fist. They'll examine the panties, looking for exactly what killed me. The coroner will think poison or chloroform at first, but they'll soon figure out that Laney's used delicates can kill a man simply by being the ultimate user experience of women's lingerie. Her black, lacy bikini panties taste like what every man secretly hopes their girl's delicates taste like.

Sheer perfection.

"I've wanted to fuck you for so long. Do you want this cock after I make you come with my mouth?" I say to the void, half hoping Landon isn't outside my door and recording on his phone. If he is, I hope he thinks I have a woman in here with me. "Such a yummy little pussy."

I buck and squirm on my bed as my hand moves over my dick in the same rhythmic touching I've done for years to rub one out. Sure, it's fun to have a partner, but I always know just how to get myself off. I've thought of Laney when I touched myself over the last decade. This time, her panties cover my face, and her taste is on my lips and just under my nose where I imagine it'll stay after I take her panties off my head. I'll be able to inhale and smell her on my skin later tonight.

I squeeze my eyes shut and clench my ass cheeks as I arch off the bed. I'm so close - like I am when I'm with a woman and not with my own fist. The difference now is the smell of Laney in my nose. My body responds like I'm Pavlov's dog after hearing the food bell.

I look through the black lace and watch my abdomen heave with my breath as I try to get control of my body. I haven't been this wild for my own hand since I figured out that it felt good to touch my dick. I throw my head back, close my eyes, and swirl my tongue over the fabric as I jerk myself. Hot pleasure moves from my balls to the base of my spine, and I whimper, breaking the silence in the room and startling myself.

I pant into the underwear on my face and imagine the loss of breath is comparable to her sitting on me. Would she lean back and finish me with her hand? Turn around and sixty-nine with me?

"Laney," I moan softly, jerking my cock faster until hot cum spills from my cock, running over the webbing between my thumb and index finger as violent spasms move through my core. My neck stiffens, and my toes curl into my blanket. "You're mine, Laney. I've wanted you for so long, and I'm never letting you go after I get you in my bed."

I can't let any other men experience this greatness. The idea of another man with his head stuck in her used lingerie makes me sick. I need to buy more. Hell, I need to buy all of them...or at least as many as I can reasonably afford. With my salary and the fact that I have a roommate and a paid-for car, that's a lot of expendable income going to the one woman I would do anything to take care of.

Let's Be Friends

LANEY

"How about lunch?" Milo asks, knocking on my cubicle frame. He leans against it in his black suit with a maroon tie knotted loosely against his neck. His hair is rumpled, and I wish I could run my hands through it just to see what it feels like and tell him I was simply straightening his hair. "My treat."

It's my first day on the job, and nobody told me when my lunch break would be. I get to eat, right? I'd like to start with a Milo sandwich, and I quickly run through the quickie lunch options in my mind. I don't mean burgers or tacos. I mean bent over a counter, up against a wall, and in the breakroom.

"Do we have time for it?" I'm not sure I'm talking about the burgers or tacos.

Fuck, why is he such a distraction in my life? It's my first day on the job, and all I'm doing is drooling over Milo when I should focus on not fucking up everything I touch.

"I think so. We're not draconian around here. There's a chili place up the street, and they give you all the saltines you can handle for the people that like a little chili with the saltines."

"You sure talk pretty with that mouth, Milo Coulson. I bet you get all the ladies with the saltines line. Either that, or you know my kinks."

Milo reddens. He actually fucking blushes. "If saltines are your kink, you need to get out more," he says. Then, he mutters something else under his breath that sounds a little like, "And I've pegged you wrong."

I slip out of my work shoes and slide into walking sneakers. Grabbing my purse, I stand and suddenly feel self-conscious with my walking shoes and pencil skirt. Whatever. This is a guy who used to regularly see me in a Bart Simpson nightgown and zit cream.

He smiles, pushing off the cubicle frame, and I follow him down the long hallway and into the lobby. He presses the button for an elevator, and we wait in silence, listening to the far-off dinging as the elevator stops at every floor.

Is it just my imagination or does he keep looking at me? Is he blushing? He didn't even blush during the "Anal Vice" incident. He's not someone who embarrasses easily, and I suddenly understand the saying *penny for your thoughts*. I'd pay a couple bucks, even in my current monetary condition, to know what Milo is thinking.

"How do you like it here so far?" he asks.

"It's nice, thank you for finding it for me and putting a good word in."

He taps his black shoes on the marble floor. "I told you I'd help, and I meant it, Laney. If you need help, you just need to ask me."

"I know. Thanks."

"How is the other income stream?"

I startle like someone just dropped something heavy next to my ear. "What?" I practically shriek.

Other income stream? Shit! Does he know about the panties? Did Samantha or Chantel tell him? Oh, fuck. Oh, fuck. Oh, fuck.

Heat sinks into my stomach, and my knees shake so much they're damn close to buckling.

"The driving app? Is that going well?"

I audibly sigh, not even caring that he probably wonders why I'm relieved he's just asking about the driving job. I steal a glance at him out of the corner of my eye, and he adjusts the tie at his collar, pulling on it like it's suddenly hot in here. Why does he look awkward?

The elevator comes, and it's crowded, so we don't speak until we file out of the elevator on the ground floor. I wait for him to hold the door for everyone as they exit, his finger on the button that keeps the door open.

When we walk next to each other, I fidget with my purse, not knowing what to say until I realize I never answered him. "Um, driving is OK. They pay on a weekly schedule, so that's nice. Thanks for asking."

"Sure," he says as we step into the street. It's an unseasonably warm day for this time of year, and he briefly tilts his face to the sun. "It's nice you have a...side gig."

Why the absolute fuck does this entire lunch seem awkward? This is Milo, for fuck's sake. Sure, I'm attracted to him, but we've never had this much trouble speaking to each other. Our sentences are short and polite like we're making small talk at a work cocktail party. What's next? The weather?

"Wow, it's warm and nice out today for winter. Great day for a walk," he says.

Something's up. "Is anything wrong?" I ask.

"Why would something be wrong?"

"Not once, in the entire time I've known you, have we ever discussed the weather unless it was hot enough to go swimming as a group. In that case, we'd only talk about who's bringing burgers and who's bringing the buns. What's going on?"

Milo opens the door to the small chili joint and shrugs. "Maybe I'm just nervous because we're working together now. Our relationship is different at work than when we hang out with our friends. I guess it's weird for me to see you as a coworker and not Landon's little sister."

I practically sag where I stand, and the air rushes out of me like a deflated balloon. Great. He only thinks of me as Landon's sibling. Will this man ever see me as a woman? I'm a sexual being. I'd love to be a sexual being with *him*. But he seems determined to keep me in the friend zone forever. I bet he doesn't even think I own a vagina. In his mind, judging by the way he treats me, I'm a doll. Not even a sex doll with holes to peck at.

A waitress in a paper hat walks by and tells us to sit where we like. Milo leads me to a booth in the back of the café, and we shuffle over the red and black tile until we're ensconced in an old booth with torn upholstery, facing each other and nervously flipping through our plastic menus.

When the waitress comes to take our order, I order a bowl of chili, extra crackers on the side, and some celery with ranch. Milo orders the same, and the waitress looks Milo up and down before walking away and tucking the stereotypical pencil behind her ear. What's it like being physically admired any time you leave the house?

"New boss being nice?" Milo asks.

"Well, compared to Wayno, he's been an absolute dream. I see why you like this company. I haven't heard a single joke involving a girl from Nantucket or any stories about the guys from the mailroom and a sheep."

"Maybe you can come on permanently at some point."

That would be nice. Working with Milo. Seeing him every single day. A flush moves up my cheeks, burning all the way up to my forehead. "We'll see. I have some virtual interviews scheduled. Hopefully, something pops off soon."

Milo clears his throat. "I actually wanted to ask you something, and you can totally tell me to fuck off."

I tilt my head. This seems interesting. "Um, what is it?"

"I was wondering if you'd like to come to our game night tomorrow night."

I rear back in my seat. Game night? Milo and Landon's game nights are notorious. They're usually packed with beautiful women and whatever big deal boss, client, or coworker they're trying to impress that month. My brother and Milo subscribe to those group mystery boxes that have you solve a murder or find out where the suspect of some tragic event is hiding. Everyone works together to solve the case while drinking only the best liquor and smoking the best cigars. It's also a big deal on the dating front. Landon introduced his last girlfriend there. It's like a cotillion to introduce special lady friends to their coworkers for the first time.

I've never been invited to one, even though I'm Landon's sister. I've often thought there's something scandalous happening over there. Orgies? Money Laundering?

"Game nights are a big deal in your house. Why am I just being invited now?" I ask, trying to sound casual. I shrug a little like I can't be fucked with going to their stupid game night.

But I desperately want to be there.

He looks down at the menu, even though we've already ordered. "We've been friends for a long time, huh?"

This is the first time he's called me *his* friend. I've always just been Landon's little sister. "Friends?" I draw out the word like I'm confused.

"Come on, Laney. We've spent a lot of time together over the years. Family barbeques. Graduations. Funerals. Weddings. I think we can call each other friends by now."

"Sure," I say, shrugging.

It's hard to stay calm when my heart pounds out of my chest, thumping so loud that I hear it in my ears. I look at Milo, wondering if he can hear it. I'm no way near cool enough to be friends with Milo.

"I guess what I'm saying is..." His voice trails away, and he wipes his forehead. Is he sweating? He grabs his glass of water and takes what can only be described as a gulp. "I guess I'd like to get to know you as *my* friend, rather than Landon's sister or my new coworker."

"Milo, you know everything there is to know about me. I'm not exactly a spy for the CIA or secretly hang gliding on weekends. You know my hobbies and my friends. What else is there to know?"

He nods and smiles. "It was just a thought. I mean, I want to...spend time with you." He fiddles with his silverware, unwrapping them from the napkin and setting them on the table like we're at a fancy event. "I'd like to spend time with you without our friends shoving beers at us or inserting commentary."

A gasp forms in my throat but doesn't come out. My eyes widen, and my pulse rockets even higher than it was. "Do you mean a date?"

Milo suddenly looks like he's being attacked by bees. He waves his hands in front of him and around his face. He shakes his head, and my soul deflates. "Not exactly." He chuckles, but it's not his kind of laugh. He usually laughs so that you can see the joy in his eyes. I only see embarrassment there. "Not a real date."

"Like a fake date?"

Milo slouches and looks at the table. For a moment, I think he's going to bang his head on it. Is he really that irritated with me?

"Not a fake date. Just...getting to know each other in a new way."

Something dark inside of me enjoys seeing him squirm. He hasn't squirmed much in his life, and the part of me that fancies itself a villain is downright gleeful that Milo Coulson is unnerved. I have no idea why he's nervous, but why not push it?

I smile and watch him take another drink of his water. "That sounds like you want something sexual."

I really shouldn't have pushed because Milo sprays water out his nose and coughs until I partially stand, lean over, and pat him on the back. "I'm just kidding, Milo. I mean...could you even imagine us, you and me, doing anything sexual? It's ridiculous, for fuck's sake."

What the hell am I saying? Shut up, dummy! I think about fucking Milo Coulson almost every time I slide my fingers down to my slit. I've thought about Milo when I was with other men.

Milo composes himself, his face still red. He smiles at the waitress when she brings our chili, and his eyes watch me as I dump saltine package after saltine package into my bowl. "Obviously nothing sexual could ever happen between us. Just, well, just come to game night tomorrow. I'll tell Landon that I invited you because you're having a hard time with work."

Fucking Landon - my only reason for not leaning over and landing one right on Milo's lips. I'd even tongue him right here in the booth. Hell, I could have been tonguing him for years if he wasn't my brother's best friend. How did my brother turn into the biggest cock block of my life? Wait. What's the female version of being cock blocked? Pussy suppressed? Beaver bamboozled?

"Have you told him that you want to spend more time with me?" I ask.

Milo's hand freezes with his spoon halfway to his mouth. "I haven't got that far. Just come, OK? We can see how he reacts to you being at game night and go from there."

"Go from there," I mumble, wrapping my head around Milo's words.

Go where? Where does he see this heading? Can I even ask that without making this weird?

I dip into my lunch, my mouth watering. I don't know whether it waters for the chili or for him. Probably both. "Sure. Friends. Game night. It sounds fun, Milo. Thanks for inviting me."

Only Murders in the Shower

MILO

I grip the white, cotton panties in my fist and pump them around my dick as I let out a groan and lean my head against the shower wall. The cool tile settles me so I can edge myself better. My chest heaves with the desire to finish, but I push it down, wanting to savor the thought of her wearing these same panties. Walking around in them on a normal day.

I hate it when I come too fast when I think about her, especially when I have a fresh pair of Laney's website panties in my fist.

Fuck washcloths and shower sponges. Thankfully, Landon and I have separate bathrooms, and he never comes into mine. He won't notice the revolving door of his sister's panties that hang from my shower caddy after I'm done with them. After they're dry, I pull them down and hide them, but my bathroom is private.

Then again, he would simply think they belonged to whatever woman I brought home last and think she'd left them in the shower. He certainly wouldn't think I was jerking off with them just to feel them next to my skin.

And I'm totally using them in place of a shower sponge. The water has cleaned them well enough, so I feel zero remorse as I lather them with a bar of soap and drag them over my shoulders. In fact, I have quite the routine down – lather shoulders and wash arms, wring the panties, lather again to wash my face and neck, then wash my downstairs bits before using them to jerk off. When I'm done, I hang them on the caddy to dry and then...

Then, I buy another pair.

I have officially purchased thirty-two pairs of underwear from Laney. They all come in basic packages and all come to my super-secretive postal box. Part of me wonders if I should buy them all at once so I can have enough for the entire month, but I like putting regular money in her hands. I like thinking that she smiles when she sees a purchase come through the site. Does she do a little fist pump or a shoulder shimmy? Does she tell Chantel she had another sale? Does she wrap it up for me immediately, all the while wondering if Billy Shitner is some maniac?

Because I am. I'm fully cognizant of that. I'm a maniac for everything Laney and nuts for her panties.

At this point, it's an adrenaline rush. Some people need Instagram likes or a video to go viral on Tik Tok to feel high. I need a basic, yellow envelope delivered almost daily with a pair of soft, lacy panties I can rub on my dick.

We all have our quirks. And I've qualified for the website punch card, now having collected three free pairs of Laney's blend.

"Yeah, Laney. Suck that fucking cock for me," I grumble soft enough so her damn brother won't hear if he's on the other side of the wall. "Use that tongue."

I speed up my thrusts because I'm aware of time. It's game night, and guests will arrive soon.

She'll arrive soon.

There is no way I'd be able to function around her like an adult if I don't rub one out first.

My breath catches in my throat, and I throw my head back as the water pulses down my body in rivulets. I open my mouth, catching water in it, and quickly spit it down my body, watching the water mixed with my spit hit the panties. "Fuck, Laney, get it wet, baby. Let me see your spit on my dick before you ride me."

And that's where my mind goes. In my fantasy, I'm in my bed on my back, Laney on top of me and rocking over my dick as she moans my name. I'd give anything to hear her call my name with my cock inside of her.

My balls tighten, and I lift my dick so the water can hit my sack and intensify the sensation in my entire pelvic region. My stomach contracts, and my legs practically buckle. I catch myself on the soap dispenser attached to the wall and curse and moan under my breath.

I cuss every foul word I got in trouble for as a kid. I say her name over and over between the bad words, willing a night with her in my shower into existence. I would do so much – push her against the wall and take her from behind, a fistful of her wet hair in my hand like horse reins.

It's the idea of her hair that pushes me over the edge, and I blink, focusing on the cum dripping from my body and swirling down the drain.

"Fuck, Laney, you rock my world."

Once I'm drained of every drop of cum, I wring the panties out, turn off the water, and hang the panties on the little hook where they'll drip dry until they're dry enough to shove under my cabinet behind extra bars of soap and old towels. Almost as an afterthought, I turn back to them as I step out the shower, lean over, and let a drop from the soaking panties drip into my open mouth.

***

"The cook was in the larder the whole time. He couldn't have done it," Landon's coworker, Daniel, says. He takes a swig of red wine straight from the bottle and crosses out the cook's name on the game card.

Everyone at the table marks the suspect off their own cards and mirror Daniel as they raise their glasses of whatever they're drinking. If I didn't know better, I'd think this was a drinking game.

I'm usually heavily involved in the game, solving it first most of the time. But I've contributed nothing tonight. I've hardly spoken a word except to ask Laney what she wanted to drink, ask her if she wants chips, or ask if she wants another slice of pizza. I'm treating her like my mother acts when I go home for Sunday dinner.

Fussing.

I need to cool it or Landon's going to notice I'm fawning over her.

It's hard for me to concentrate on the mystery we're solving tonight because Laney's thigh is right next to mine. An inch away under the table. The one inch makes my skin itch like I need her pressed right up next to me or my skin will break into hives.

"Are you having a good time?" I ask, turning toward her enough to see her but not face her. She nods but is otherwise quiet.

Landon squints at us from across the table. "Why is she here again?"

"Rude," I say, not looking up at him. I'm afraid he'll see the lust in my eyes. Lust for his sister. "I invited her since you won't invite your own sister after years of living in the same town. I work with her now. Be nice."

Good. Turn it around on him being a rude asshole and don't draw attention to the fact that I'm a lovesick puppy.

Laney sits quietly at the table as we draw clues in turn and share with each other round-robin style. We make notes in our notebooks quietly and eventually break off into teams to do research and investigation for the case. Laney's not on my team since Landon made the teams.

Does he suspect something? Is the fucker cock blocking me?

I glance at Laney out of the corner of my eye, and she quickly turns her attention back to her own team. She turns her head so fast that beer from her cup sloshes onto the decorative scarf around her neck. It's sopping wet, and she unwinds the fabric before dropping it onto a dining room chair.

She. Was. Staring. At. Me.

Does she feel the same about me as I feel about her? Does she suspect I have ulterior motives for inviting her tonight? Does she suspect I'm Billy Shitner since I can't stop staring at her lip gloss? I have no idea why I think that would tip her off, but I can't help but be paranoid I'm going to be found out before I get a chance to do more than hold her panties after I buy them. I want to slide them down her legs, wad them up, and throw them on my floor before I spread her legs and...

"Yo, Coulson!" Landon practically yells, clapping his hands in front of my face. "Are you looking at my sister?"

The room goes silent, and Laney turns to me, blinking. Everyone stares at me and then, almost in perfect unison, slowly turns to Laney. Her face reddens, and heat creeps into my own cheeks.

I should deny it.

Deny.

Deny.

"Um, yeah. I was admiring her...lip gloss."

Fuck all. I didn't deny it. Laney tilts her head to the side like she's seeing me for the first time.

Landon has an almost twin expression of confusion on his face. "Her lip gloss? You into lip gloss now?" he asks.

I shrug. "It's shiny. Like..." My voice trails away, and I wrack my brain for something to compare her lip gloss to. "Like shiny marbles."

Someone just bury me now. If the universe could open up a sinkhole under my house and suck everyone that heard this conversation into it, that'd be great.

"Do you want to wear my sister's lip gloss?" Landon asks, close to laughter.

I want to wear it on my lips when she kisses me, and I very much would like to see if it similarly shines on my dick, but I can't say that to Landon. "Sure. I'm secure in my manhood. You aren't?" I turn to Laney, put my hands on my hips, and give her a chin nod like absolutely nothing is wrong. "Can I borrow your lip gloss?"

Her eyes flick around the room and the amused faces. "Um, I didn't bring it. It's at home."

I put my hands on my hips. "That's a fucking shame. It's gorgeous. Looks good on you."

Landon looks at Laney and then back to me, his brow creased. "Right." He draws out the word as people stare at the entire interaction.

I don't look away from Laney. No matter how much I want to look away because of embarrassment or scrutiny, I don't. If I don't start showing her I like her, and that I have liked her for years, this will never progress. I'll be permanently friend zoned. She'll eventually find someone that won't treat her nearly as nice as I dream of treating her. She'll get married to that dick, and I'll sadly shuffle to the wedding with a toaster. I'll have to clap and act happy when she has children with another person someday.

Fuck that shit.

Fierce possession, the likes I've never felt before, sends heat through my chest at the thought of Laney pregnant with another man's child.

The room is still silent as people sip their drinks and focus more on Landon and his reaction. I hold the contact with Laney's eyes and don't even blink once. "You look beautiful tonight. I just thought you should know."

The air practically crackles with tension as Landon frowns, a slow smile forms on Laney's face, and I clap my hands and turn back to my mystery team. Eventually, people focus on the game again, but I know this will be the talk of the group tomorrow on text messages and by water coolers. At least, it'll be hot gossip for people that know us well.

"He was obviously killed with blunt force trauma," I say to the woman next to me who's, unfortunately, not the woman I want it to be.

Losing Scarves...and Panties

LANEY

I blow on my hands and flex my fingers, trying to warm them before knocking on Milo's door. Footsteps finally sound from the other side, and he swings the door open.

Fucking God. Did I wake him?

Gray sweatpants sit low on his hips, and the outline of his dick is in front of my face since there are a couple of steps up to the door. A weird gurgling sound comes from my throat, and I force my eyes away. Looking at his face isn't much better, though. Stubble dots his cheeks because it's late, and his hair is messy. He runs his hands through it slowly and pats it down.

I check my watch. It's after ten. "Uh, sorry it's so late, Milo. I was driving someone home from the airport, and I realized I left my scarf here on game night. I thought you'd be up." I jerk my finger over my shoulder in the direction of my car. "I'll let you go back to sleep."

Milo smiles and holds the door open, stepping back so I can come into the condo. "I dozed off on the couch for a few minutes, but I'm up now."

"Sorry." I step into the house and take stock of the two empty beer cans on the coffee table along with a half-eaten slice of pizza on a paper plate. "Is it self-love night?"

I cringe and close my eyes before the last word is even out of my mouth. Did I just ask Milo if he was masturbating? I blow out a breath and try not to sound crazy. "I meant that it looks like women do when they're depressed. The pizza and the beer."

Milo crosses his arms and leans against the wall. "That's the difference between men and women, huh? Pizza and beer are considered a happy and normal thing for us. Ice cream, too. Women think they should only let themselves enjoy food when they're depressed or have somehow earned it."

"I'm not depressed, and I definitely like food."

"One thing I like about you." He reddens after he says it and rubs the back of his neck. "I mean, I like you for more than your ability to eat."

"Good to know," I say, laughing and trying to put him at ease. I look around the living room. "Do you have my scarf? I think I left it here."

Milo walks to the apothecary table in the corner of the room and opens a drawer. He pulls out my perfectly folded scarf. Did he iron it?

"I washed it since you spilled beer on it." He holds it out to me, smiling the sexiest smile in the world. "For you."

Our fingers touch as I take it from him. Our fingers have touched several times in my life. Passing things to each other at Thanksgiving friend celebrations. Playing cards. Buying rounds of drinks. This feels different somehow.

This feels dirty.

His eyes darken, and my knees shake in response. They're like gelatin when his eyes are dark. I can't think. I can't make any decision other than deciding that he's the most handsome man I've ever seen.

He leans forward, catching me before I faceplant into the table. We stare at each other for several moments, my ears ringing with the deafening silence of the room. My stomach flutters at his touch, and his finger comes to my chin, tilting it to look up into his eyes.

I expect him to say something. Call me clumsy. Laugh at me for falling over when he hands me a scarf.

But he's not laughing. His jaw flexes, and his eyes flick to the door. Looking for my brother, perhaps? When the door doesn't swing open, he inches closer to me.

Closer.

Closer.

Holy fuck, is he going to kiss me?

My eyes widen, but I don't move. I won't. I'm going to stand my ground and not run away from Milo kissing me. If I continue to run and dance around the fact that I very much want him to kiss me, it'll never happen. I'll have to watch him marry a blond woman named something like Trixie with political school board ambitions. I'll have to watch him have children with Trixie and probably even go to her baby shower, where I'll take a box of diapers and a set of environmentally friendly baby dishes.

I take a deep breath and let whatever's going to happen...happen.

His mouth is on mine, and his lips are warm. Slightly wet, like he never needs Chapstick. He probably doesn't. I mean, he's perfect Milo. The simple feel of his lips intoxicates me, and my neck lolls back like I'm a ragdoll while Milo cups my face.

The kiss is soft at first. His nose grazes mine as he tilts his head to the right. He pulls back and says my name in a husky voice, almost as an apology, before I reach up and pull his face back to mine, desperate.

He smiles against my lips but accepts the hungry kiss. His tongue slides against my teeth, and I open more, allowing the intrusion. Allowing him to search.

His hands move from my face and down my body, stopping at my waistband. Scandalous thoughts run through my brain, but his hands are respectful. Even though they're respectful, there's still the promise that they'd be very *disrespectful* if I gave him the green light.

I grip his shirt and pull him to me harder, and he backs me into the wall. The light kiss from a few moments earlier is gone as we hungrily kiss so that my spit is in the stubble surrounding his mouth. Are we making up for lost time? Has he wanted to do this?

I open my eyes and glance at the beer cans on the coffee table again. Only two. He's not drunk. This isn't a pity kiss or a drunken mistake. Milo wants to kiss me. I can tell by the...well, his pants situation.

My eyes flutter shut at the erection pressing into my abdomen. His dick is hard and so close to me. It's hard *for* me. I'd never in a million years think this could happen.

His arms leave my body and box me into his space against the wall. He pants as we kiss, breathing heavily through his nose as I run my hands everywhere I can reach. Those broad shoulders. Down the cut abdominals I can even feel through his shirt.

"Laney," he whispers again before pushing his lips so hard against mine that our teeth touch.

I push him back a little. "Tell me this has nothing to do with the two beers on your table."

"Oh, it certainly does not." He moves his lips to my neck and pulls my hair with one hand, tilting my head back against the wall so he can reach my collarbone. "You smell so fucking good."

I assume he's talking about my neck, and I nuzzle the side of his face as he licks, kisses, and nips at me.

"Come upstairs with me," he whispers, working his way to my jaw. "Landon could come home."

"You only want to take me upstairs because of Landon?"

"Fuck no. I want to go upstairs anyway, but I don't want him to see us. But if you're adamant you don't want to take this to my bedroom, I guess we can do whatever you're up for on the couch."

Fucking hell. He wants this to escalate. My body shakes. My stomach drops like I'm in an airplane that dropped altitude, and my clit practically screams at me to do something. Say something. Move.

Then I remember the situation I'm in.

"I can't d-do anything," I stammer, my heart pounding in my chest. Just a glance at his forearms boxing me in has me undone.

"Laney," he sighs. "Let this happen between us."

"I'm on my period." I squeeze my eyes shut. Fuck, I just told Milo about my period. Can I crawl into a hole now?

He's my brother's friend, and I've known him forever. Come to think of it, I flash back to freshman year when Landon and Milo decorated my room with my unused maxi pads, sticking them on my walls and hiding in my closet to watch my shock and embarrassment. It was a juvenile prank performed by boys. I was mortified then, and I'm mortified now. He'll push away from the wall. He'll tickle me under my armpits, tell me this was all a big joke, and walk away. We'll laugh about it the next time we all hang out. At least, *he'll* laugh. I'll be mortified until I'm forty.

"Well, I guess that sixty-nine session I've fantasized about is off the table tonight, huh? But periods don't stop a good pounding," he says, placing such a sweet kiss on my forehead that I expect him to walk away again.

But he doesn't leave. He stays in my space and dips his head, nuzzling my neck with his face and dropping warm kisses on my exposed collarbone. "I still want to make you come so hard that you cry," he whispers.

I freeze, and my mouth goes dry. I can't speak. I can't move. I can't do anything but let him kiss me while I rub my thighs together at the idea of sharing a body, no matter how briefly, with Milo Coulson. What would it be like to let him touch me everywhere? The area of my ribcage under my breasts trembles with the idea of his mouth or hands on it. Hair on every part of my body stands on end.

I let him lift me a little and let him tuck his face into my neck, breathing in my scent. I let his hands move my legs so they're wrapped around his waist. I let him walk us up to his room and close the door behind him, and I let him lay me gently on his bed, climbing over my body until we're facing each other in the dark room.

It all feels surreal. Like it's happening to someone else. I pinch the skin on my forearm when he's not looking. Who comes over to their brother's house to pick up a scarf they left and ends up having hot sex with the man they've fantasized about for years?

Only a sliver of moonlight comes through the window, and I study his expression above me as he studies mine, caressing my face as his eyes roam over my skin. He was hot when we were younger, but his jaw is more pronounced now that he's in his early thirties, and I trace my own finger over his growing stubble.

This man above me is the same one that I grew up with and has seen me at my worst – my most real. He's the man I threw a badminton racket at when he played too aggressively at a family barbecue. He's the guy that drove me and my freshman-year boyfriend to a movie when my parents couldn't. He's the guy that I ate ice cream with on the curb of my childhood home more than once. I think he even paid for me to get a Choco Taco from the ice cream truck a time or two when I didn't have any allowance money left.

He's also the man that's about to fuck me stupid if the look in his eyes is any clue.

He still wants me. He's still hard against my thigh, and the imposter syndrome that's stirred in my stomach whenever I'm around him, telling me I'll never attract a man like Milo, slinks away. He clearly wants me if his heaving shoulders are any indication. He controls his breath and pushes his tense, muscular thighs into his bed like he's stopping himself from humping me.

I tremble as he lifts the hem of my shirt, and his fingers dance across my stomach. He lifts me a little off the bed and pulls my shirt over my head. My arms tense in the cold air, and he notices, rubbing his warm, masculine hands down my arms before moving his hands to my jeans. "I'm going to undress you. Do you need a minute in the bathroom?" he asks, dropping kisses on the skin around my bra strap.

"I just use the period underwear."

He pulls back. "Period underwear?"

"Yeah. It's newer. It absorbs and you just wash it." Oh, my fucking God, did I really just use the word *absorbs* to explain my period to Milo while he's trying to fuck me? Why not just tell him how *moist* I am for him? There are two words you never use around a man you're trying to fuck, and I just used one of them.

My face reddens, and I hold my breath and wait for him to laugh or crinkle his face in disgust.

Instead, he shrugs. "Interesting." His mouth moves back to mine, and I melt into our kiss until he pulls back. "Hold that thought, though."

Milo gets off the bed and disappears into his attached bathroom. A few seconds later, he comes back to the room holding a red towel. "Lift up," he directs, and I do what he asks.

After the towel is down, I open my arms, and he settles his body back onto mine, propping his head in his hand next to me as he idly traces his finger between my breasts. "I don't suppose I've ever told you that I've wanted to do this for a long time, huh?"

I cover his hand with my own and roam my body with him. "You have?"

"Does that shock you? That I've thought about you this way?"

"For how long?" I ask, squinting. Just how perverted is Milo Coulson?

He chuckles at my inquiry. "Relax, Wyatt. It was around the time you were twenty. You were just different. I saw you as a woman and not Landon's bratty sister."

"I can still be a brat." It comes out before I can stop it. Who am I right now?

He smiles a naughty grin. "We'll see about that."

Milo dips his head to my breast. He nuzzles the fabric of my bra out of the way and takes my exposed nipple into his mouth, sucking hard and making my eyes flutter as he flicks his tongue over the nub. He moans slightly, and my hand comes to his hair, fisting it as he draws my nipple into his mouth hard. This isn't simply breast appreciation. His sucking is meant to consume. I'm certainly not lactating, but if I was, Milo would get mouthfuls of me. He latches onto me hard, and my legs move open into a butterfly position. "Milo," I moan.

He comes off my breast with a popping sound and swirls his tongue over my nipple as he looks up at me. "If I can't suck on your clit tonight, this will have to do, Laney."

"Do you, uh…" My voice trails away, and I clear my throat. "Do you want me to suck on something of yours?"

Shit. I'm not a virgin. Why do I sound so utterly inexperienced and timid? I'm an idiot.

He moves up my body until his mouth is at my jaw. "Would you like to put your filthy, little mouth on something of mine? Because I want that very much. I've thought of you on your knees for me."

Warmth moves through my body and all the way to my feet. My mouth waters at the idea of Milo's cock in my mouth and moaning my name as I unman him. I've thought long and hard about how powerful I'd feel with my head between his legs as he unloads into my mouth.

Somewhere inside of me, the tiger I only unleash on occasion comes out, and I push Milo so he rolls to his back. His hand cups my cheek as I attack him. I breathe in his scent – woodsy with a hint of sweat. I actually fucking purr as I lift his shirt and run my fingers over the abdominal muscles I've wanted to touch for over a decade. He bites his lip as my hands move down his body and stop at his drawstring.

I make quick work of untying his pants, and I take a deep breath, preparing myself. I, Laney Wyatt, am about to learn how big Milo Coulson's trouser monster is. I blink twice to wake myself up if this is a dream. If it is a dream, I'll roll over and go right back to sleep to see if I can jump right back into it, like I'm jumping into a body in that old show my dad likes, *Quantum Leap*.

I drag his pants down, and he lifts his butt a little to help me undress him. He breathes through his nose, controlling his body.

He really shouldn't bother because I feel him tremble. His shoulders heave, and a drop of nervous sweat trickles down his chest.

And I find a fucking anaconda between legs as I pull his boxer briefs down.

I rethink my ability to even put his cock into my mouth, but I've never been a quitter. I'm not going to quit now that Milo's dick is literally in the palm of my hand.

He throbs as I slide my fingers over him. I wipe a drop of wetness away with my thumb and move down his body until my head is nestled between thighs so muscular they could crack walnuts at Christmas.

I look up at him one last time, and he meets my eyes. "Suck my dick, Laney," he begs. "Please."

I've never heard his voice shake or sound unsure. This is a whisper. This is him giving me control of his body and pleasure. Power moves through my body, and I lick my lips one last time before I draw my tongue up the underside of his cock, flick my tongue over the spot men like just under the head, and swirl my tongue over his tip as I look at him and bat my eyes.

His hands fist my hair, and his butt immediately clenches. His back comes off the bed, and he throws his head back with a curse.

"I'm sorry. Did you like that?" I taunt.

"Satan," he says, his lip curling into a sneer. "Suck it or let me fuck you. Stop dicking around."

"Dicking around, you say?" I run my tongue down the underside of his cock again and move my mouth to his balls where I suck on one as hard as he latched to my breast earlier. I come off it and lick the ball next to it to introduce myself. "What was that about a dick?"

"Laney," he groans. He swirls his hips like he's searching for my mouth, bucking into my face. "Baby, please."

Baby? I'll play nice if he's going to call me that.

I take as much of his dick into my mouth as I can take without gagging. I can only get about halfway down at my deepest with sucking just below the head being a happy medium. If he's butthurt about only taking him that far, he doesn't show it. If anything, he accepts whatever I give him with gratitude, if the cuss words filling the room are any clue.

I look up at him as I devour his cock. His head is thrown back, and he's propped on his elbows. Fuck, he's sexy as hell when he's being undone.

And he lets me undo him. There's a piece of me that's shocked by that. I was always Landon's kid sister, and Milo always put on the show of the cool brother's best friend. He's not cool now. He's a man getting his dick sucked and showing the woman sucking it exactly how much he likes it. He's allowing me to see him broken and in rapture.

He rocks into my mouth as his cock hits the back of my throat, triggering my gag reflex. "Laney," he growls. "Fuck, Laney, I'll come too fast if you keep going. Come up here."

I take his dick out of my mouth and jerk the base as I squint. "You don't want to come in my mouth?"

"I want to come in every hole you have, but there's one I've wanted for way too long."

It's deadpan. The words hover in the air over us like a cartoon bubble. "I've never had a guy stop a blow job before," I whisper as Milo grabs me under my armpits and slides me up his body.

"Believe me, I've never stopped a blow job. But you can drink me down another time. I've been waiting for something for years, and I'm going to fucking have it tonight."

He rolls me onto my back and kisses me hungrily, unconcerned that his dick was just in my mouth. Some guys don't like the idea of that, but Milo doesn't care. He runs his lips against mine and dips his tongue inside my mouth, catching my bottom lip gently with his teeth.

He pulls my jeans down my legs and kisses my shins and knees as he comes back up. He makes sure I'm positioned over the old towel and pulls my underwear down.

Please don't look at them. Please don't look at them.

He pulls the underwear off and drops them over the side of the bed where I can easily grab them when we're done. It's like he knows what a woman needs at this point. He doesn't look, giving me the privacy of my messy underwear.

His legs nudge my thighs apart, and embarrassment seeps through me. I've never done this on my period. Ex-boyfriends weren't interested, and I was too self-conscious to offer. "It's fine, Laney. It's not a big deal. I can still make it feel good," he says, pushing my legs apart because I hold them stiffly together in shame. He leans over me, kisses me on the forehead, and gets back on his knees, his cock positioned at my entrance. "Let me drive. And it's going to feel so fucking wet for m e."

His eyes are dark and hooded. He's obviously not bothered. His dick isn't softening, and he isn't running away. He doesn't tell me to put my underwear back on and go home.

He grips my hips and pulls me down onto his cock, impaling me in a swift and glorious movement.

We both grunt at the feel of the other. He swivels his hips in a circle as he gets me used to his size, but the extra lube helps me take his length. "Milo," I squeak.

His hand splays across my lower abdomen, holding me in place, while his thumb sets up shop on my clit. "OK if I stay on my knees for a while?" he asks.

"W-why?" Fuck, I can hardly talk.

"I can watch every muscle twitch, every facial expression, and kiss your legs if I want. I also get to rub this clit and make you lose your shit before things get too good for me."

I arch my back and close my eyes as I rock into his thumb while Milo makes good on his promise of kissing my leg. He pushes in deeper as he throws one of my legs over his shoulder and places a kiss on my knee. "You're fucking gorgeous, Laney. You feel so good around me. Don't be self-conscious. This is just me. Us. Take what you want."

His thumb is magic. My core trembles with pleasure as he's relentless in his ministrations. He knows just how to touch me. I push aside all thoughts of the other women he's practiced on to get this good at thumbing a clit because he's thumbing mine now. That's all that matters.

His eyes are closed, and his other hand is everywhere – my pelvis, my thighs, and my legs. His fingers graze my leg at the same time he pushes a little more pressure on my engorged nub at the center of my body, and I shatter. My vision tunnels. I moan his name. My pussy convulses around him as he cusses at the feel of it. I'd give anything to see what his expression is as he watches me come, but I can't see anything but pinpricks of light as they dance across my eyelids. "Milo," my voice squeaks, and I'm breathless. I'm surprised I could even say his name. But it's the only name I've ever wanted to say while overwhelming pleasure moves up and down my body.

When I'm done, he leans forward and wipes hair out of my face. I don't know how it got there and why it's sweaty. I wrap my arms around him, and his back is already wet with exertion. A drop of sweat rolls off his face and lands just above my lip. I quickly lick it, letting the salt roll over my tongue as he speeds up his thrusts. "Wrap those beautiful legs around me, Laney."

I do as he asks, reveling in the feel of his muscular body between my thighs. I'm unhinged and buck up to meet his every thrust. Fucking Christ, if my brother is a block from home, he'll hear every word and every moan as Milo fucks me so hard the headboard hits the wall. Very bad words that are completely inappropriate for public use come out both our mouths with every thrust, and I grab Milo's firm ass. I've always joked that I could bounce a quarter off his ass, and the way he clenches his butt as his own orgasm builds tells me I was right about the quarter.

"I didn't even ask, but do you like to be fucked rough or gentle? I've always wanted to know," he says, out of breath above me.

"Hard. Dirty. Slut." Those are the only words my mouth forms. Grammar and sentence structure be damned.

He chuckles against my jaw. "Laney Wyatt likes to be fucked hard like the dirty, little slut she is for me?"

"Yes," I whimper as one hand grips my throat and the other pulls my hair a little.

"Mmm. I think we're going to get in the shower after this, and I'm going to push a very bad little girl up against the wall and fuck her from behind. Is that what she wants?"

"Fuck, yes!"

"Yeah, I think you're mine tonight, Laney. All night."

I arch into him, pushing my breasts against his hot skin, and he loses control. He thrusts into me hard, so hard I'll feel him tomorrow. Maybe that's his end goal anyway, but mission accomplished. He holds my throat and pushes his lips to my cheek to mutter filthy things as his orgasm tears through him. I've always wanted to make him come, and I'm making him come so hard that I may have lost hair from his exuberance.

He releases inside of me with a groan, and I let his cock drain of every spasm and twitch, my legs still wrapped around him. He nuzzles my neck and coos, his breath slowly evening.

This is where he'll get up, playfully smack me on the butt, tell me it was fun, and I need to go home. This is where it'll all just be a fun shag as his remorse about fucking his best friend's sister will punch him in the face.

I don't expect a kiss on my collarbone, a kiss lower on my breast, and then his hand is in mine. He leads me to the shower and hands me a towel, also red. He turns the water on, waits for the temperature to heat up, and pulls me into the shower with him.

"You're here tonight," he says, whispering. "Stay with me."

"Are you sure it's OK?" I ask. Letting the warm water wash his cum and my blood down the drain. He doesn't look at it, giving me the privacy to clean myself.

He squirts some body wash in his hand and runs it up my center, cleaning every part of the area he just tore to shreds. "Did you think I was going to push you out the door like a one-night stand?" he asks, kissing my jaw. "Not you."

As he turns me around and cleans my butt the same way he just cleaned my pussy, I wonder how long he'll want me.

Could this be a real thing for us, or am I just the new forbidden toy?

This is Awkward

MILO

"Hey," I say a little too loudly.

Laney startles and spills hot coffee on her blouse. We both reach for a tissue on her desk at the same time and blot at the wet spot. I also grab the bottle of water bottle by her laptop and unscrew the top, ready if she screams that the coffee's burning her. Not that soaking her shirt is the way to go. We're at work – not at the local bar's wet t-shirt night. I watch the stain blossom on the pink fabric.

Pink fabric...like the panties I ordered from her yesterday. Sure, I've now felt the real thing around my cock, but I can't stop ordering her underwear. I want to see, feel, and taste every pair that comes through that website. There's also a little of me that wants to support her. I get an adrenaline rush when I think about touching anything belonging to her, but that doesn't compare with the elation at the thought that I'm helping her out. Being her hero in some way.

Thank fuck Landon stayed at a random woman's house the same night Laney stayed over. I snuck Laney out at six in the morning and missed Landon by ten minutes. It was a close call.

Laney's face reddens with either embarrassment about our night together or pain from the coffee. Hopefully, it's the coffee that has her not looking at me as she dabs herself. I want her to be proud of us the other night. I don't want her to regret it like it was a drunken shag or that we did anything wrong.

"Milo, you scared the shit out of me."

I purse my lips and think of something to say that could truly dazzle her. I've talked to thousands of women on the spot and have wooed them with witty banter. Why do I have such an issue coming up with something to say to her? Fear of rejection?

"Fancy seeing you here." I cringe after the words come out. Great. I sound like an eighty-year-old woman. "Just thought I'd come by and see how you are. You left in a hurry the other day."

She tosses the tissues in the trash and sighs, looking at her shirt and realizing it's toast. "I didn't want to run into Landon. How are..." Her voice trails away and she closes her eyes, shaking her head like she wants to restart the conversation. "How was the rest of your weekend?"

"Good," I say, sitting in the small chair next to her desk. "I would have liked to have made you breakfast. Can I do that sometime this week?"

"Breakfast?" she asks.

"Eggs. Bacon. Biscuits or pancakes. Your choice on that. The first meal of the day."

"How would that work with Landon as a roommate?"

"OK, I'll take you to breakfast."

She smiles a weak grin and blinks. "Do you mean a date?"

"No!" I say, and her face falls. Part of my heart swoops to see that she's disappointed because I don't think of it as a date. The other part of me hurts that she could possibly think I don't want to date her. "Breakfast isn't a date. Breakfast is bonding time after waking up together." I pause and take a deep breath. "But I'd like to take you out for a real dinner, Laney. Just us."

She pulls her shoulders back, and something lights up in her eyes. "You would? Me?"

"Why do you say it like that? I want to take you on a date."

I scoot the chair closer to her. Her desk phone rings, and she looks at it like it's a snake. Something that's ruining a big moment for her.

Is this a big moment for her?

She smooths her hair and collects herself, completely ignoring the phone, even though it rings again like it's an important call. "Should you get that?"

"Probably," she says, deadpan. "What did you say about a date?"

"Let's go out. Officially. Maybe a nice dinner and hanging out after."

She looks down. Fuck. She doesn't want to go out with me. The other night was just sex to her. A fun roll in the hay. I thought it was something special to her, too. Did I get my vibes crossed? How does she put me so far off my game? I'm usually a pro at being able to tell if a woman wants to marry me by the second pump or if she's not feeling it.

My stomach flutters with nerves I haven't felt since I asked Jenna Godrick to the movies in seventh grade. That's the last time I remember being nervous about asking a woman to spend time with me.

I blow out a deep breath. She's worth it. I'm going to just bite the bullet. I also need to know, once and for all, if this was just a simple shag. "Maybe we should talk about the other night."

Laney's eyes widen, and she stands up from her chair so suddenly that it rolls back and hits the filing cabinet. Grabbing my arm, she looks both ways coming out of the cubicle and marches me to the room next door to the printer where we store print paper and coffee filters.

She shoves me through into the small room before I can protest and closes the door, clicking the brass lock so we won't be interrupted. "Why did you ask that at work?" she asks in a harsh whisper.

"What the hell, Laney? If anyone overheard me asking about the other night, they'd just think it was a conversation or some other drama. They wouldn't know we had hot sex!" I pause and lower my own voice to a whisper. "It was hot, right? I didn't imagine that?"

She rubs the back of her neck. "Um, yeah. It was definitely hot."

"Let's talk about it. We didn't get a chance in the morning."

She looks back at the door, worried someone will catch us in here. She probably should have thought about how it would look for both of us to creep out of the paper closet together, but there's no way to prevent that now. "What's there to talk about?"

I've never been a big feelings guy, but I have to bite my lip and give this hell. "Laney, I want to talk about how you feel about it. We've known each other a long time, and you're my friend. I want to make sure we're OK. If we're not, I want to *make* us OK."

She shakes her head a little and reaches for my tie. Before I can grab onto anything or think about the consequences of doing this at work, she yanks my tie, pulling me toward her. My head points down before I can stop myself, and her lips are on mine. She's wearing heels, so she doesn't have to stand on her tiptoes like she normally would for us to kiss, but I still wrap my arms around her waist, pulling her even with my lips.

Our tongues find each other, and we're suddenly not in the copy paper room at our janky office job. We're somewhere far away where we won't be caught at work or by her brother. A beach in Mexico with the wind rustling through our hair. A garden party with swans nearby. That's where she should be kissed. Not a copy room.

I cup her face with my hands, melting into the kiss, but she pulls away first. "Do you really mean that, Milo?"

"Mean what?" I ask, my eyes still closed and very much hoping she'll put her lips back on mine.

"Did you mean that you want us to be OK?"

I lean my forehead against hers, and it feels...right. Like my face has belonged glued to hers all along. "I want it to be more than OK. Let's go out and see what happens. One date. One date to see if we can hit it off as more than friends."

She pulls away from me, and my face instantly feels cold. Abandoned. "What if it doesn't work? Fuck, Milo, what if we end up pissing each other off or hurting each other? I won't be able to hang out with you again. No more beers with friends. No more running into you at dinners my family has. It'll hurt us both. Maybe it's best if we both walk away while we can."

Like. Fucking. Hell. I just got half a chance with her. I'm not walking away from anything.

I steel myself for rejection and tilt her face up to mine. "Look at me."

She averts her eyes and stares at a ream of paper at her eye level. "I can't."

"Look at me."

When she finally glances into my eyes, she blinks twice until she realizes I'm not looking away. We're hypnotized by each other. There is no one else in the world. "Do I look like I'm fucking around or planning on hurting you?"

"N-no," she stammers.

"Give me a chance to prove to you that I want to be more than friends. If you think the other night was just a fuck, I'll throw up my hands and walk away. But if there's a chance that you felt what I felt with those legs wrapped around me, go out with me and give this a chance."

"What about Landon?" she asks.

"What about him?"

"What if he finds out we're going on a date? He'll go nuclear."

"Then we won't tell him. At least, we won't tell him right away. He doesn't need to know anything. Besides, we should make sure we like each other enough to spend more time together before we announce it. We'll keep it quiet and then deal with telling him if we have to make it public."

"I don't like keeping things from him."

"He's your brother. Aren't siblings supposed to keep things from each other? Lie? Kick each other?"

She smiles and finally breaks eye contact, looking at the floor and shuffling her feet. "Um, you mentioned something about feelings when my, uh, legs were wrapped around you the other night. Just out of curiosity, what did you feel?"

Using my body, I push until her back hits the wall with a light thud. Her shoulder hits the light switch, and we're temporarily blanketed in darkness until I graze my fingers over her blouse and turn the light back on. I lean against her jaw and place a light kiss on her earlobe before whispering, "I felt your warm pussy shatter around me."

"Besides that."

"I felt like I actually shared something special with someone for the first time. I know you won't believe it, but I've used a lot of women for physical need over the years." She wrinkles her nose and doesn't chuckle at my sarcasm. "But what happened the other night felt like more. It was...emotional. If it wasn't a big deal to you, that hurts me, but I need to tell you how I feel. It felt like the most natural thing on the planet to do that with you."

"I know."

I cock my head and smile, trying to meet her eyes. "Yeah? You felt it too?"

She gives a short nod. "It was definitely different from what I experienced with, um, other guys in the past. There was something there." She suddenly looks up at me with a horrified expression. "Milo Coulson, don't you dare tell me this is a prank to get me to vomit feelings you have no plan on returning! This isn't a joke, right? You have a hell of a history of tricking me for a laugh."

I lick two of my fingers and smile before reaching down and sliding my hand up her skirt. When I reach her lacy panties, panties I know I'll search for and buy later tonight, I part her slit and circle my fingers on the spot she went nuts for the other night. I reach over her shoulder again and turn off the light before checking the lock on the door. "Does this feel like a prank, Laney?"

Basketball Bust

LANEY

"**I**s the wine to your liking, sir?" the sommelier asks, stopping by our table and greeting Milo with a little bow.

I've never been on a date with Milo, but I can't help but wonder if everyone is like that with him. Do waiters always nod their heads in compliance when he asks them to take away the extra silverware or waves in the direction of his water goblet?

For the first time, I wonder if I really know every side to Milo. We're comfortable as friends, but I've never seen the customer service side of him like I see on most first dates. Every time I've been out with him in the past, we've been at a bar, a chain restaurant, or pizza place after a night of bowling or rec league softball. Come to think of it, one or both of us wear sweatpants any time we're in the same place.

Milo swishes the wine around the glass before inhaling to check for...well, I have no idea what people check when they sniff wine. I'm more of a *just give me the closest thing to fruit punch* kind of girl when it comes to wine tasting. He brings the glass to his mouth and takes a tiny drink. "A hint of cherry," he says, smiling at the sommelier. "This will be fine."

"Of course, sir." The man pours us two glasses of the chosen wine and places it in the container at the edge of our table before walking away, wringing his white-gloved hands.

"Sir," I imitate.

Milo rolls his eyes at me. "Somewhere along the line of our time knowing each other, I became a sir. You just didn't notice."

I look around the restaurant, one I've never been to, and marvel at the tapestries. The fact that the place has tapestries tells me all I need to know.

I can't afford this.

At least, I can't afford it on my company salary. I can probably swing a salad on what's left of my website money this week.

But Milo doesn't know anything about me selling my panties. Can he smell my anxiety?

My armpits sweat, and I tap my toes in my scuffed ballet flats that suddenly feel low class for a place like this. I lean forward, trying to ignore the heat moving up my neck when I realize I have ten dollars of cash in my purse, and I'm not entirely sure I picked up my debit card off my bedside table before I left the house.

I paste on my best smile for Milo. He deserves that. "This is a really nice place. Have you been here before?"

"I bring clients here. I've always thought it would be a great place to bring a date, but I never have."

I nod. Well, that's something. Milo doesn't bring an army of women through here. I take a deep breath and open my menu, determined to enjoy this properly.

I touch my silverware, mentally working out which fork goes with which course. Looking at the menu again, I clear my throat. "The salads look wonderful here. Have you had them?"

Milo flops his menu down in frustration and pinches his nose. "Stop. This is my treat. Get what you want. I only see you eat salad before you have a seven-course meal. Don't piss on me and tell me it's raining. Get the steak or scallops I know you want."

"No," I say, shaking my head. I look back at my menu, weighing the option of cranberry pecan salad or grilled chicken with avocado.

His warm fingers settle on my own. "Laney, let me buy you dinner. I want to. I need to do this for you. Let me feed you a meal. Please."

"I wouldn't feel right about it, Milo. We're friends, and we should split it."

Milo withdraws his hand and smooths the front of his shirt. He exhales and smiles as the waiter approaches the table to take our order.

I order the cranberry and pecan salad.

"We'll have the calamari appetizer to start," Milo says, smirking over his menu. "I'll have the steak, but please bring an order of scallops to the table for us to enjoy with it."

The waiter looks between us, confused. "You want two entrees, sir?"

"Yes. I'm starving. Can you also bring some of your truffled potatoes for us to share? Thank you." Milo folds the menu and hands it to the waiter without breaking eye contact with me.

I shake my head and wrinkle my nose. "Separate checks," I grumble.

"Of course, ma'am."

The waiter walks away, and a blush creeps up Milo's face. He fumbles with his own silverware and looks around the restaurant until something behind me catches his eye. "I'm going to go to the restroom. I'll be right back," he says quickly, not looking at me.

As soon as he leaves the table, I let out a sigh. I'm really fucking this up. I just don't want to feel like I owe him anything, even though I plan on riding him like a prize stallion later, and I don't want to feel like I can't buy my own meal. I'm proud that I've always supported myself and covered my own bills and food.

Should I let him pay for my scallops, though?

Milo comes back to the table and sits in his chair, pleased as punch at something. I look behind me to see if I missed something happening, but I only find the normal wait staff deliveries and the hostess leading an elderly couple to a table. Are they clients of Milo's or something? "What are you smiling at?"

"Nothing. Let's chat about what we're doing the rest of the night."

I straighten in my chair. "Well, St. Bart is playing Westcott for the state title. Want to watch some basketball?"

His mouth drops open slightly, and I smile. He gets up again and circles the table, taking my face in his hands and rubbing his nose against mine before kissing me square on the lips. I look around the restaurant as people stare. They probably think we got engaged.

He pulls away from my face, and I laugh. "Is that a yes?" I ask.

"I've forgotten about our shared love of basketball. I was down for a movie or something, but that sounds better."

We talk as we work our way through our appetizer, and I allow myself to enjoy a few bites of it. Maybe it'll appease Milo into not worrying about me only getting a salad. We talk about people we know, my parents, and his dad's retirement plans. It all feels comfortable with no awkward questions because we know each other so well. It's like I'm Cinderella and the shoe fits.

Maybe the shoe has always fit.

When our food comes, we eat in silence, and Milo pushes the scallops toward me. "I'll just throw them away if you don't eat them, Laney."

"You wouldn't dare waste them like that."

He leans forward and licks his lips. "Try me. I got them for you. Let me give you something to enjoy."

My face reddens because I think Milo has given me plenty to enjoy lately, but I tentatively spear a scallop, popping it into my mouth under Milo's watchful eye. He's probably making sure I actually eat them.

As soon as the scallop hits my tongue, I close my eyes. The butter they were cooked in is a perfect complement to the tender meat, and I let out a small whimper.

"Good?" Milo asks, picking up his steak knife and cutting his steak. "Better eat them all just to make sure the kitchen didn't fuck them up."

And I do. I eat every last one, even considering picking up the plate and licking the seasoned butter.

When we're finished, I look around for a staff member. "We should probably get the check and head to the game. Where's the waiter?"

The waiter appears as if I'd summoned him from my words and walks straight to Milo, not even meeting my eyes as I hold up my finger. "Your card, sir," he says, handing Milo a credit card.

"Ah, thank you. The meal was delicious." I look at Milo as my mouth drops open, watching as he puts his credit card back in his wallet. "Now that the bill's all handled, let's get going to the game."

***

"I insist!" I say, nudging Milo out of the way at the box office. "It's five bucks each. Let me do this, Mr. Sus Scallop."

"Dear God, don't let that be my new nickname. People will think my dick's the size of a scallop."

I spin to face him and smile an inch from his face. "Keep tricking me to pay for things, and I'll tell everyone it's true."

"So, you'll tell everyone you're very familiar with my dick?" he asks.

"Well, not yet," I say, smiling and handing my ten-dollar bill over to the teenager. She takes the money and puts it into a metal money box before stamping our hands. "But we'll eventually have to tell people something if this continues."

Milo and I walk to the home team's side and find a spot a little out of the way. The game is busy, but it isn't packed. Most of the students sit together further down the bleachers, while parents and faculty sit in the upper section. We sit on the first bench of the parent section, and Milo helps me out of my coat.

As soon as our coats are off and under our butts, Milo grabs my chin and turns my face to his. "I haven't kissed you as much as I'd like tonight, and I'd like to make it known we're here together."

"Why?" I ask, my eyes glancing at the people around us.

"I don't want anyone to think you're available or that I'm your brother. I want everyone to know you're my date."

His lips hover a centimeter from mine, and his breath smells like the wine we had for dinner. I run my tongue over my lips, already salivating for a taste of him. "Are you trying to pee a circle around me?"

Milo smiles as he presses his lips against mine. He's soft and controlled at first, and he runs his nose against mine before leaning to the right and deepening our kiss. My hands move to the back of his neck, and his skin warms my cold fingers.

"Laney?" a voice asks above us.

Milo and I both freeze, and our eyes simultaneously pop open.

"Laney Wyatt?"

I move my hands away from Milo's neck, and they're instantly cold again like I'm not inside under an HVAC system. Looking up, a face comes into focus. Dark hair. A plain face with childishly chubby cheeks. Messy hair and old sweatpants.

"Colin Krueger?" I ask, my voice shaking.

The man smiles and puts his hands on his hips as he runs his eyes over me. He then looks at Milo as I squeeze my eyes shut for a moment.

Fuck. Fuck. Fuck.

Colin is friends with a mutual friend of Landon's. Does he know Milo?

They must not have met because Colin simply chin nods at Milo in the way guys do when they don't know each other but need to politely acknowledge the other's existence. Milo looks between Colin and me like he's watching us play pickleball, his eyebrows raised. Questioning.

"Hey, Colin. I didn't know you liked basketball."

How fucking stupid am I? Most guys my age in Minnesota like basketball. It's one of the only sports they can play year-round inside. Even my voice sounds like I'm desperately clinging to a random conversation topic to avoid the elephant in the room.

Either way, Colin ignores the question. "Is Landon here?"

Milo's eyes widen a little, and his head jerks in my direction.

Think, Laney. Diversion mode. Change tactics. "Nope," I say, clapping my hands and pasting a smile on my face. "He's got something else he needed to do, so it's just me and my...friend."

Colin chuckles and looks at Milo. "Yeah, you look all kinds of friendly."

The gods smile upon me because Milo opens his mouth to speak just as another man, probably Colin's father or uncle, taps him on the shoulder and holds up two hotdogs. The other man smiles at Milo and me and nods to a spot higher up in the bleachers.

Colin looks at me one last time. "Good running into you. Tell Landon I said hello. Sorry to interrupt you and your...friend."

I wave and Milo gives a small thumbs-up sign as Colin follows the older man to their spot on the bleachers and unwraps his hotdog. As soon as they get settled, both Milo and I exhale deeply and stare straight ahead. No kissing. No touching. Our hands go straight to our laps.

"Sorry I didn't introduce you. Colin is best friends with Brandon who works with my brother. I only know him from Landon's four-person golf scramble we did a year or so back. I don't think you were able to play, so I joined my brother's team."

"I know Brandon. Never met Colin, though. Do you think he'll rat us out to your brother before we're ready?" Milo asks.

"Nah, he's a good guy. Works in IT or something and usually doesn't talk to many people. I'm not entirely sure why he hangs out with Brandon. Brandon isn't exactly one of Landon's nicer friends."

Milo nods and slides his hand back over to mine, and I wind my fingers through it. "Don't let him ruin our night. Who cares, right?" I ask.

Milo looks at me out of the corner of his eye and grins. "I care, Laney Wyatt. I care a lot."

I'm not sure if he's talking about caring about me or caring if Landon finds out we went on a date.

Lover's Lane

MILO

"My place or yours?" Laney asks, and my mouth waters at the words.

"Yours," I say, playfully pulling her side braid. "Landon has a couple of people over. We can't sneak upstairs without them noticing if that's what you're wanting."

She runs her hands up my chest, and I lean back, looking left and right to make sure none of our coworkers are walking down the cubicle aisle. "That's what I want," she whispers. "We didn't get our lunch fun today."

I had a meeting and couldn't sneak off with her. We've been fucking around at lunch all week. Even if it's not full sex, it's something – lots of kissing, hand jobs, or oral for me. It's easier to whip my dick out in my car than it is for her to spread wide and let me really get into it. Landon's been around the house, so I haven't been able to have my way with her.

I'm insatiable when it comes to this woman. I can't get the taste of her lips out of my mouth and the smell of her hair out of my nose. If I think I'll forget, there she is again, rubbing her hand up my chest or cupping my face.

And when she's not around, I sniff her panties more than any sane person should.

"I was kind of joking when I asked and was hoping you'd say we could go to your place. We can't go to my house," she says. "Chantel's parents are in town. Their flight got in an hour ago."

"I can be quiet," I say, nipping her earlobe and eliciting a chuckle from her.

She looks at the cubicle next to us and covers her mouth. "No, you can't."

I smile and pull her close for a long hug. I get a hint of her body wash and her laundry detergent. Things that are...Laney.

I reach for the purse on the hook next to us and hold it out to her. "Are you ready to leave? Let's go for something to eat and then go for a drive. It's a nice night for late winter. Snow's coming again later this week, and I want to enjoy the night while I can."

Laney squints. "Are you driving me to a make-out spot, Milo Coulson?"

"Tacos first. Then making out."

Fifteen minutes later, Laney fumbles through the hot bag of tacos on her lap. She unwraps one and bites into it while we're stopped at a red light. A stray piece of shredded cheese rests on her lip, and I lean over, grabbing it with my tongue.

"That's mildly gross," she says, laughing and wiping away the spit my tongue left.

"Why? I've kissed you a hundred times this week alone. Hell, I came in your mouth at lunch yesterday."

The light changes to green, and I hit the gas pedal a little harder than I should, desperate to get to the quiet parking spot where I know we'll have a great view of the night sky and won't be bothered. I'm taking Laney to my secret spot – the place I take women to impress them for picnics or night viewing.

"Still weird to eat off my face, Milo."

I smile to myself and take a right turn as Laney continues eating. She chews and looks out the window as I turn down a side road and then find the reflective stake that marks a gravel lane. She looks up at the trees rising from both sides of the road and wads up the food wrapper before reaching into the mega box of tacos and handing me one.

I set it on my lap and place my hand back on her thigh. That's where I like my hand when I drive now. When she's not eating, she usually places her hand on mine and idly traces the veins of my hand. It's become a habit. So much so, that I put my hand on Landon's thigh the other day by accident when I drove him to pick up his car that he left at a bar.

I apologized and told him it was a habit. He raised his eyebrow, a quiet way of asking who the fuck I've been fondling while I drive. I could hardly tell him that my hand wanders over to his sister's leg.

"Are you taking me out to the wilderness to murder me?" Laney asks.

I pull my car into the clearing atop a hill, and Laney takes a deep breath through her nose as the entirety of Minneapolis appears below us. Even my breath catches like it does every time I come up here at night. It's gorgeous.

But not as gorgeous as Laney.

I put the car in park and finally let go of her leg, needing my hand to open my food and eat. "Murder you? The only thing I'm going to murder tonight is these tacos...and then maybe yours."

Laney laughs, and a little taco shell comes out of her mouth. She wipes the spittle on my dash with her finger. "Murder my taco? Are you in high school?"

I smile in response, and we eat in silence, staring out the windshield and watching the lights of Minneapolis, mesmerized. When we're done, we both get out of the car like the skyline has invisible strings, pulling us toward the view.

We circle the car, and Laney leans on the hood. When I start to lean next to her, I suddenly remember what I have in my trunk and leave her for a moment, a confused look on her face.

"I have this in my trunk. Want to sit on the hood?" I ask. "Remember when we used to do this to your dad's car?" I ask, spreading out the blue flannel over the grill.

"I remember," she says, letting me get the fabric settled and then heaving herself onto it. "I also remember you borrowed your dad's truck a lot. I remember watching fireworks in the truck bed one Fourth of July." She leans back on her elbows. "Aren't you coming up?"

I shake my head. "Comfortable?"

Laney lowers herself onto the blanket and hums a little. "Warm. The engine's still hot."

I pull her up, quickly lifting her and wrapping my arms around her. "Is it hot? Did I burn you?"

She laughs. "No, Milo. It feels good. The blanket's thick, so it's cozy. It's a nice night, but it's still chilly. Come closer so you can be warm."

I place her back on the blanket and run my hand down the center of her chest and down her stomach. She quivers when I get to her belly button, obviously knowing where my hand will wander next.

"I haven't had a chance to taste you. Can I have a lick?" I ask, my eyes on hers as she looks down and runs her hand through my hair as I lower my head.

She looks around at the trees surrounding the clearing. "Here?"

"I've come up here since I was a kid when I wanted to get away," I say, placing another kiss after moving her waistband down an inch. "I've never seen another soul. The only living things watching are raccoons or owls."

I lift the hem of her shirt and press a kiss to her stomach as my fingers fumble with her work pants. I have them unbuttoned and unzipped in short order and pull them down her thighs. Pressing my body to her legs to keep her warm in the night air, I study her underwear.

Yellow with red roses on them. A little lace along the leg holes. A single embroidered rose at the waistband.

I'm also aware she's tense and shaking from something that isn't cold air. "Do you not want me to go down on you?" I ask. "We don't have to do anything."

"No, Milo. I want to. I just...I've been working all day and haven't had a shower since this morning."

Fuck, why are women like this? Why don't they understand we don't want a perfectly clean box to snack on? What kind of man wants to eat a woman only when she's perfectly showered? I like pussy to taste a little earthy with a smidge of salty sweat on it. Why do women worry so much about it? If everything's healthy and you wash once a day, I want to taste it. Bury my face in it.

"Laney, if you showered this morning, it'll be exactly the level of filthy I want. I want to taste your day on you."

"Really?" she asks, crinkling her nose.

"Stop being so self-conscious about something every time we're together. Did I ask you to get your pants on and go home when you were on your period?"

"No."

"Did I laugh at you?"

"No."

"And I'm not going to judge you now. Relax and let me move these cute little panties to the side or I'll eat you through them if that's what I have to do."

She hesitates, still worried.

But I meant what I said, and it wouldn't be the first time I sucked on her dirty panties. Not that she knows that.

When she thinks, I push my face into her core and swipe my tongue over the yellow fabric, making a show of closing my eyes like I'm savoring her. "Yummy," I say when my tongue reaches her waistband.

She grips the hair on the top of my head. "Milo."

I growl and dip my head to her pussy again, lapping at her underwear. My tongue moves over her clit, and I smile against her. A wet line forms in her underwear, and I don't know if it's from my spit or her own excitement. Probably both. "When you're ready for me to stop fucking around, you'll have to tell me."

"You want me to beg?"

"Yes," I whisper, dipping my head again. "If this drives you nuts, let me eat you for real. Just slide them an inch to the right, baby."

Without a word, she lets go of my hair and moves her panties aside, revealing her wet slit. It practically glistens in the moonlight. That could be my imagination, though. I've wanted to taste it for so long that I may be putting a mental halo on it. The epitome of pussies is in my face, and I get to taste it for real. Not her dirty panties.

The real prize.

And it feels like a prize. Everything about this feels like I won a million dollars. I hungrily take a leisurely lick up her center from pussy to clit and wrap my lips around the throbbing bud, sucking on it and flicking my tongue over it at the same time.

Her legs close around my head, and I revel in it. She brings me closer to her body and holds me in place. It's all I've ever wanted for the last decade. The only noise in the field is the wet sound of spit and her arousal and the far-off hoot of an owl. Her eyes are wide when I look up at her, but she doesn't watch me. She looks at the sky and the pinpricks of light above us as steam leaves her mouth every time she exhales.

My own breath speeds up as every flick of my tongue and every movement of my fingers over her skin lifts her ass or arches her back. As shy as she was when we first started, she's clearly over that. She squirms into my mouth and bucks against me, fucking my face without an ounce of shame.

This is what I wanted. I've wanted to undo her. Hear her moan my name because of something my tongue does to her.

"Milo," she moans.

She's so lost in her pleasure that she slides down the hood a little. I catch her hips in my hands and hold her in place on the car so she won't fall, and I steady her as she rocks and squirms against me. My back aches from leaning, but I keep licking her clit, knowing it'll be my turn soon enough.

"Right there," she moans, holding my head in place as I suck around her clit. "Fuck, Milo. Holy shit."

She shatters, and it's the sexiest thing I've ever seen or heard. Her voice echoes in the open space as her moans bounce off the trees around the clearing. Her body shakes, and her feet grapple against the edge of the hood like she's not sure what to do with them. Wetness coats my tongue as I lick and lick through every second of her orgasm and even a minute afterward as she fists my hair.

I kiss my way up her stomach and lift her shirt enough to move her bra out of the way and lick her nipple. It practically quivers under my tongue.

I kiss my way further up her body, unbuckling my pants as I go. "Mind if I take a turn?" I whisper into her neck.

"Please," she whines, shimmying a little and angling for my cock as soon as it's free of my pants.

There's no fumbling or fussing. No worry about whether she wants it or not. She's warm, wet, and ready for me as she kicks her leg out of one of her pant legs and hooks it against my left ass cheek. In the cold air, I welcome her warm leg back there, and I push into her body with a groan.

She arches her back and whimpers as I pull out a bit and ram home again, standing over her as she takes every inch of me. My legs practically buckle at the feel of her, but I mentally chastise myself. I will not fall over in front of her because she feels so fucking good. I'm not a teenager. I'm a sexually experienced man in my thirties who's fucking a gorgeous woman on the hood of my car.

I thrust back and forth as she moves her hips to meet me, and she runs her hands up and down my forearms while I hold her hips. I bite my lip so hard that I taste blood. "Laney," I moan. "Is this what you wanted all day?"

"Yes," she whines, squirming under me, her neck lolling.

"I wanted this all day. It's all I can do to keep my hands off this body at work. And this pussy..." My voice trails off as I take deep breaths through my nose, controlling the orgasm building in my balls. I'm going to have to think about baseball to keep from being labeled a two-pump chump.

She clenches my dick with her pelvic floor, and all thoughts of baseball go out the window. I speed up my thrusts, an unhinged madman as I grunt her name, bad words, and something that doesn't make a bit of sense. I'm a mumbling idiot.

Tears roll down the sides of Laney's face, and I stop, gasping. "Did I hurt you? Why are you crying?"

Laney curls up, grips my ass, and pushes her forehead to my chest. "It feels so good. Fuck, Milo, don't stop! Why are you stopping?"

I push her back again and cover her body with my own as I lean over the hood. Something gives under us, and I wonder if I'll have a small dent from both our weight on it. I'll pop it out later because the only thing I care about right now is pleasing her.

More tears roll down her cheek, and her muscles tighten as I get close. "You going to come with me, sweetheart? We going to come together?" I ask, cooing the words.

She throws her head back, and I swear to God her eyes roll. My own eyes flutter as I reach the pinnacle of all human pleasure. She shakes and moans under me as my load fills her own wet core.

When I'm done, I cover her body and let her wrap her arms around my back to keep me warm because I can't pull my pants up yet. I can't bring myself to pull out of her. I want the connection.

I want to do this more. Much more. But how much more will she allow? And what would she think if she knew I'm going to go straight home and buy those panties with the roses on them and revel in my own spit on them when they slide out of the package?

Money Dump

LANEY - TWO WEEKS LATER

"I need your expert advice," I say, dropping my purse at the front door and not even stomping the snow off my boots.

Not that Chantel gives a fuck. Apparently, she can't be fluffed with even looking up from early episodes of *Drag Race*. Her feet are in slippers and propped on the coffee table. She's taken a page out of my book and is already in her pajamas at eight at night. In the past couple of weeks, it's like we've traded bodies. I've been out with Milo almost every night, and she's been at home in her pajamas and her terry cloth bathrobe like we've swapped bodies or personalities.

She hasn't asked questions about where I've been, and I'm confused by her lack of curiosity. I'd be a little nosy if she didn't come home most nights. Granted, I've texted her and told her I had a little too much to drink and was crashing at Landon's so she wouldn't be worried. That's not unusual, except for the fact that it's been several nights. She probably just thinks I'm on a depression bender.

And I'm not lying about where I'm sleeping. I'm just leaving out that I'm in Milo's bed every night. In addition to the basketball game, Milo and I have seen most of the movies that are out, tried three new restaurants, and even went bowling. I beat him by a few pins, but I think he let me win.

"What the fuck is wrong now?" Chantel asks, gesturing toward the television with her popcorn bowl like I can't see she's watching something.

"Nice way to talk to your roommate who has a problem."

"Did your online underwear store get shut down?"

"Ha. That's not even funny. I'd be out three hundred bucks a week if that happened."

She straightens and widens her eyes. "You're making three hundred a week on that?"

"Is it still funny? Are we still laughing about it?" I ask, sarcasm dripping from my voice.

"No, we are not. I'll be making an account later. I'm eyeing that trip to Costa Rica."

"I have a bigger problem." I chew on the inside of my cheek. "But it kind of goes along with the underwear site."

Chantel puts the popcorn bowl on the couch cushion next to her and leans forward, her eyebrows invisible under her bangs. "Why do I have the feeling this is going to be some good shit?"

"I've been seeing someone, and I'm worried they'll find out I sell my panties."

I hit her with it point blank. Once the words are out of my mouth, I grab the abandoned popcorn bowl and slink onto the other end of the couch as Chantel makes a face I imagine she used on Christmas morning as a child when she received an especially outstanding present. "Is that where you've been every night?" she asks.

"Yeah. I've been with him." I throw my head back on the top of the couch. "It's insane, and I think...well, I think I love him. In fact, I know I love him. And I'm getting laaaaiiidddd."

"That good, huh?" she asks, taking back the popcorn bowl with a selfish grab. "Details or no popcorn. How can you love a guy you just met? You've only been out for two weeks."

"Because I haven't just met him." I look at her out of the corner of my eye, gauging her reaction. It's good practice for when I tell my parents.

Or my brother.

Chantel clears her throat. "How long have you known him?"

"A long time."

"Anyone I know?" she asks, shoving a popcorn kernel into her mouth. She chews for a second while I weigh saying Milo's name. Once I spill the tea, I can't put it back in the cup.

I take a deep breath and blow it out through my nose. I can't keep him hidden forever, and it's smarter to have him stay at my house instead of me over there. Milo's had to sneak me upstairs like we're fifteen or something so my brother won't see. It's also getting a little hard to keep getting up at five in the morning to sneak out so Landon won't catch me creeping out of Milo's room.

"It's Milo."

I expect her to choke on her popcorn or something. I face her in case I have to lean over and give her the Heimlich maneuver.

Not a blink.

Not a sniff, gasp, or even a cough.

Silence hangs between us, and I wave my hand in front of her face like she may have had a brain freeze or something. "You aren't shocked?"

"About time you two started doing the dirty. Everyone and their brother knows you've wanted to for years. Well, maybe not *your* brother. He's blissfully ignorant." She puts another bite in her mouth. "Ooh, does Landon know?"

I shake my head. "What do you mean you've known we wanted to hook up?"

"Oh, please. It's obvious from the way he looks at you."

"How does he look at me?" I ask, genuinely perplexed.

How did I miss this? How the fuck did my friends know and not tell me? For fuck's sake. I could have been with him for years if someone had given us both a heads-up that we were into each other.

Chantel sighs with annoyance. "The same fucking way you look at him. It's annoying as all hell. Googly eyes. Actually, his eyes light up and do this weird focusing thing when you walk into the room." She looks out the bay window behind me with a small smile. "It's like he doesn't see anyone or anything else when you're in the area. He looks at you like I'd like a man to look at me someday."

"Like he wants to fuck me?"

"Oh, no," Chantel gasps and puts her hand on her chest. "Well, I mean, that's implied. He's probably waited a long time to bend you over and take you like an animal. But it's more than that."

"Explain."

"Surely, you know what I mean."

"I really don't. Explain it to me like I'm an idiot."

"He looks at you like you're the sun in his solar system and everything revolves around you when you're with him. You're the peanut butter to his jelly. The cheese to his crackers. The turkey to his holiday side dishes."

"He's had a lot of side dishes over the years. How did you know he felt like this?"

"Because he's never, not once, looked at another woman like he's looked at you. If I saw him take home a woman from the bar, his eyes were cold and bored when he looked at her, regardless of if he smiled through their conversation." Chantel places the popcorn bowl in her lap and places her hands on either side of her legs as she sits cross-legged. "Those other women had one serious problem."

"What?" I whisper.

"They weren't his best friend's little sister."

I flop back so hard that the throw pillow under me tumbles off the couch and hits the floor. I bring my forearm to my forehead like I'm an old movie actress and let my head fall back. "I have to stop selling my panties."

"What the hell for? You're making three hundred bucks a week. You're paying your bills. He doesn't need to know shit about how you pay your bills."

I wrinkle my nose. "So, if you ever start dating someone, you'll never tell them how you earn your money? I don't know, Chantel. This feels a little weird."

"Come on. It's not like you're doing something that could potentially harm his health or cause a jealousy issue. There's nothing unsafe about selling your underwear. It's a need-to-know thing, and I don't see a scenario when he'd need to know that."

I bring my legs up to my chest so that I'm curled into a ball. "I think it's wrong to start a relationship with dishonesty."

Chantel blows out a breath that ruffles her hair. A small piece of popcorn flies out of her mouth and lands on her pajama pants. "There's nothing dishonest about leaving something out. You're not actually lying. Christ, Laney, the rest of us learned this as children. Don't tell him, especially if things are going well."

I get up from the couch and sulk up to my room without another word to or from Chantel. If she's shocked by my relationship with Milo, she doesn't show it. She turns the volume up on the TV a few clicks and goes right back to eating her popcorn like she never heard the news that two people from her friend group are together.

I shut my door and crouch to the ground, reaching under the bed for my panty stash. I unwrap the shopping bag I keep the clean panties in and pull out a green bikini pair with the tags still on it. Peering at it, I breathe through my nose, trying to calm myself before I do what I have to do.

I can't send these to Lloyd Biggins in Idaho. I can't send them to Billy Shitner. Both of these men, along with a few sporadic sales around the rest of the country, have been paying my bills. I wonder about Billy Shitner, especially. He purchases several pairs a week and has bought extra stock the last few days, almost like he knows I'm seeing someone and is trying to claim my underwear as his first from the other side of the state line. If I stopped selling my underwear and shut my shop down, would he be disappointed?

Do I care what he thinks when I have my own concerns and Milo's feelings to consider? Would Milo think this is gross and that I'm sad to sell my underwear in the first place?

Shame roils through my stomach for the hundredth time as I look at these panties. I rub the fabric between my fingers and consider my options.

I should just talk this through with someone. Before I can stop myself, I reach into my pocket and pull out my phone to talk it through with the guy who's really my best friend. He's been my best friend for longer than I realized.

Text to Milo: "Hey, we know all there is to know about each other, right? At least about the big stuff."

Text from Milo: "Um, I guess so. Why? You know about the "Anal Vice" song, and you know I took two women to prom. You once threw up in my pool while making a whirlpool. I think that's a pretty good baseline. Are you having second thoughts about going out with me?"

Damn. I forgot about the pool when I threw up during a group whirlpool. I must have wiped that from my memory bank, and I'm surprised Milo even speaks to me, let alone fucks me.

Text to Milo: "No second thoughts!"

Text from Milo: "Is it Landon that's freaking you out? I have a bag of lye and a tarp if he'll be a problem. Fucker has cockblocked me for the last time."

Text to Milo: "What if we don't know everything about each other, though? What if there's something we both have that's a secret, and we're too ashamed to tell the other?"

I don't see the dots that signal he's writing. Nothing. Shit. Time passes, and I shake my phone to make sure it hasn't died. I glance at the clock app and realize it's been three minutes since I sent the text. Did I scare him? Does he think I'm up to something illegal? I better clarify.

Text to Milo: "Nothing too weird. Just more embarrassing. Ha! Totally talking in what-ifs, you know? Maybe I am freaking out about Landon."

Dots

More dots.

Dots for *a really* long time. Is he writing a book? Writing something and then deleting it?

Text from Milo: "OK."

There is no way it took him that long to write two letters. He has something to hide, too. Something he was writing in a manifesto and was going to tell me. Either that, or he wrote a diatribe about Landon going to fuck himself if he didn't like Milo's relationship with me.

I tap my fingers on the floor and stare at my phone. I should tell him. I should just tell him that I have resorted to selling my underwear and that a guy in Idaho and a guy in Wisconsin buy almost my entire stock for whatever sick things they use them for. I should come clean and get it off my chest. This is Milo. He won't care.

But what if he does? What if he's embarrassed to call me his girlfriend if I have an account I use to sell my underwear? Milo dates women who wear nice clothes and get their hair cut at expensive salons. They're doctors and lawyers. One a few years back worked for NASA, and they broke up when she moved to Houston. The women Milo dates don't sell their dainties to men in Idaho and Wisconsin.

Text from Milo: "Just know that whatever you're ashamed of, it wouldn't matter, Laney. Is there something you want to tell me?"

My fingers hover over my phone, and I suddenly understand why he took so long to answer. I want to answer in two-letter words, too. I type the words, telling him I sell my underwear, and then erase them. I do that twice before I respond.

Text to Milo: "No."

Text from Milo: "What if I have a huge secret?"

Text to Milo: "Do you have one? I'm all ears and on the edge of my seat to know what awful secrets Milo Coulson hides."

More dots.

Five minutes pass this time, and I almost get up to brush my teeth for the night. Finally, when I'm on the verge of tears and think Milo's going to tell me he doesn't want to see me anymore, my phone dings.

Text from Milo: "No, sweetheart."

I slide my legs into green panties that'll either end up in Lloyd Biggins's stash or on Billy Shitner's floor. I step into pajama shorts and wash my face, disoriented in my own bathroom since I've been staying at Milo's for the last several days. I can't remember when I last used my own electric toothbrush instead of the pink extra toothbrush that Milo fished out of a drawer. I turn off my bedside lamp with only one thought on my mind.

It's obvious Milo is also hiding something.

Sharks and Shitheads

MILO

"And then I pulled this fucking shark out of the water," Brandon says, slapping Landon on the back. Brandon's always been a blustery asshole, and when Landon said he was meeting us for drinks, I rolled my eyes. The guy grates on my nerves. "It was huge!"

The only people more annoying than Brandon are Brandon's friends, and I silently cross my fingers under the table that he's not bringing any tonight. I can't take more pretentious deep-sea fishing stories.

Landon moves his attention away from Brandon. "How was your day, Milo?"

I shrug. "Usual." I don't tell him that usual now means snogging his sister in the print paper storage closet or shoving a quick sandwich down so I can spend the rest of my lunch fucking his sibling in her car. "Laney and I had lunch."

Fuck, yeah, we did. She's been wearing more skirts for easy access when she can ride my dick for a few minutes.

I can't get enough of her. Her body. Her taste. Her smell. You'd think I was just obsessed with her physically, but that's far from the truth. I love hearing the words tumble from her mouth when she says smart shit like talking about an article she read in *National Geographic*. We played *Clue* for hours the other day on a rainy Saturday, and I couldn't get enough of her laughter. And she always figured out the case first. Then again, I was paying more attention to her than Miss Scarlet or Professor Plum. Sometimes, I forget we've been playing that game since she had braces and I was still jerking off into socks.

Then again, I'm now jerking off into *her* panties.

Another voice sounds over our heads, and Landon turns to greet the new guy. He looks oddly familiar, and I tilt my head, trying to place him. He's wearing black glasses, a rumpled dress shirt, and slacks. He looks like any guy you'd see on the street, and I scrape my brain to remember where I saw him.

Thankfully, Landon remembers his manners. "Colin, this is my old friend, Milo. Milo, this is Colin. He works with me."

I shake the man's hand, and his eyebrows move together, obviously recognizing me too. He points at me. "I know you. Basketball game."

Fuck. This is the guy that Laney saw at the game. We've met. I didn't recognize him with the glasses. How could I be so stupid? He's not exactly Clark Kent.

"I think you may be confused, man."

"You were with Laney."

The table goes silent, and Landon takes another sip of his beer. When he's done, he swallows and looks at me, confusion written all over his face. "Did you and Laney go to a basketball game without me?"

"Yeah, they did," Colin says. "Looked pretty cozy. Hands all over each other. I thought I was going to have to pull him off her face."

I literally see the words rattle around inside Landon's brain. I shake my head at Colin, my eyes wide, silently telling him to shut the fuck up.

"Laney? My sister? Are you sure, Colin?"

Colin has the good grace to realize he just fucked me straight up the butthole. He slouches down to his seat and straightens his shirt. "Um, well, maybe I was mistaken. Must have been a different guy."

Landon's eyes ping pong between Colin and me. I'm not a classically trained actor, but I do my darndest to straighten my face into an innocent expression. We stare at each other for seconds, neutral expressions on both our faces.

Eventually, Landon scoots his chair back from the table, takes another sip of beer, and places his napkin on top of his half-eaten plate of hot wings. "Alley. Fucker. Now."

"What? Is that English?"

Landon stands and grabs the front of my shirt, fisting it. "Alley!"

"Holy shit, are you two going to fight?" Brandon asks, a wry grin on his face.

"Shut the fuck up, Brandon!" Landon practically growls. "You're not invited to this party."

Landon jerks me out of the chair, and I hold my hands up, signaling I'm not going to take a swing at him no matter what happens. "You can't be serious that you want to fight me in the alley over me kissing your sister."

"Did you do more than kiss my sister?" he asks, letting go and stepping back a little so I can answer.

I pause and put my hands on my hips, looking at the floor. "I don't feel like that's your business. She's a grown woman."

"Oh, my fucking God. You smashed my sister!" He runs his hands through his hair. His eyes are wide, and his face reddens into a manic expression. "You fucked my baby sister?"

"She ain't no baby now."

Wrong thing to say. Landon spins me around, grabs me by the back of my shirt with one hand and the waistband of my pants with the other, picking me up and walking me from the bar with a strength I, quite truthfully, had no idea my best friend had in him.

Eyes watch us leave, but something about the look on Landon's face keeps people in their seats. Phone cameras turn in our direction, but not one person intervenes.

I'm frog marched down the hallway that leads to the alley and pushed through the steel back door. I steady myself against the brick wall of the building next to the bar and turn around...right into Landon's fist.

The punch knocks me on my ass, and my nose breaks. Blood splatters down the front of my shirt, and I look at my best friend, hoping he feels some remorse for punching me. Judging by the look on his face, he doesn't feel a lick sorry.

"Do you want some more?" Landon growls, his fist raised.

A little of my blood drips down one of his knuckles, and I push off the ground, ready for more. I take a deep breath, wipe the blood away from my nose, and stand up to take another hit. "Go ahead. I'll take another one."

I half expect him to be shocked by my willingness to take another punch, but he swings hard, hitting me in the jaw. I stumble to the side with the punch and then right myself. He squints and hits me with a cross on the other side of my face before I can recover from the first blow.

"You fucking bastard," he sneers. "Fucking my sister. My best friend, my ass." Another punch hits my chin, and I stumble back, falling and checking to make sure my bottom teeth are still in my mouth.

"Will you feel better if I tell you it's not fucking and more like making love?" I ask, half laughing at the stupidity of my best friend hitting me.

"No, you fucking idiot. That is not better."

I push myself up again, wobbling a little as I stand. "Are we going to talk like adults, or are you just going to kick my ass all night?"

He looks to the side and blows out a sigh before turning his eyes back to me. "I'm going to kick your ass all night."

A laugh bubbles up from my chest. I shouldn't laugh since there's nothing funny about the fact that I don't know how I'll explain my face to work tomorrow. They'll think I joined a boxing club or got into a bar fight. I have a meeting tomorrow, and I'll have to go like this. Maybe I'll even tell them the truth – that the brother of the woman I love challenged me to the 2024 equivalent of a pistol duel over her virtue.

It's worth it, though. *She's* worth it.

"I'll kill you, you son of a bitch," Landon huffs, stepping forward and flexing his hand. My face hurts, but I also know it hurts to punch someone. We'll both be icing something in another hour.

"I love her," I say, holding out my hand and hoping it stops him. It just comes out. I haven't even told Laney yet. There's no denying it anymore, though. The words felt good rolling off my tongue.

Landon doesn't hit me again, but he grabs my collar. "You think that'll get you off the hook?"

"I won't fight you if you want to keep hitting me, Landon. I'll take it and never swing back at you. I'll take it for her because your sister is the only woman I've met in my entire miserable life that's actually worth a beating. Fuck up my face if you must." I wave in the direction of my chin, panting. "Fuck it up so your sister will find me unattractive. Whatever, man. You'll still be my best friend in the world, and that sister of yours will still be the one woman I want more than anything in the universe. Nothing you can do will ever change that. You can't beat that out of me."

He shakes me a little by my collar. "I'm sure going to try, asshole."

"Fine. Go ahead. Get it over with."

He stares at me and grinds his teeth. His lip curls, but he drops his fist. "Why her? Of all the women you could have, why do you insist on my baby sister? You could have any woman you want, but you had to stick your dick in her."

"She's special. You have to see that."

"You fucked my baby sister!" he yells, holding onto my shirt and shaking me again. Some blood runs out of my nose, and I can feel my eye swelling as I try to focus on his face. "What the hell were you thinking?"

Now would be a really bad time to mention his baby sister has panties that taste like pumpkin pie and likes to be choked when I ride her hard. "I'm sorry if that hurt you," I mumble. It's the best I can come up with right now that won't get me killed.

He roughly lets go of my collar, and I stumble again. This time, I catch myself on the brick wall behind me. "I'm not worried about you hurting *me*, dickhead," he growls. "I'm worried about you hurting *her*. You're a womanizer."

"We both are," I say, gesturing between us. "You're no saint, Landon. Does that mean that you can't have something real if you find the right woman? Are you never going to find a woman to love because of your past?"

"Why her? Why? I want to know why!" he yells, sounding so much like Sally Field in *Steel Magnolias* that I purse my lips together to keep from laughing.

I pull my shirt up over my nose to catch the running blood. "Why wouldn't it be her, Landon? She's amazing. I've considered your family my second family for most of my life. She's always been there. Most of it was in the background, but she was always *there*. She's beautiful. She's sassy. Fuck, man, she's the bravest and scrappiest piece of work I've ever known. She has bigger balls than both of us combined. Maybe you should ask yourself why any man *wouldn't* fall in love with her?"

Landon runs his hands through his hair. "God, please tell me this is recent and you haven't been fucking her all along when we were teens."

I hold my hands up. "I never touched her. I thought of her as your spoiled little sister until I graduated from college and we were both adults. I swear to Christ I never touched her or thought of her any other way than a friend before then. Something changed around that time." I look at the alley wall behind him, searching for my words. "She became confident and her own woman. I want that. I want a woman who can be her own person. I want a woman who *can* do whatever she has to do to make her dreams come true. Then, I want to swoop in and make those dreams come true for her. I want her, man. I want her with every fiber of my being. It's not just my dick that wants her." I clutch my chest like I'm trying to keep my heart in my chest. If I can't have Laney Wyatt in my life, I may as well just rip it out in this alley and toss it into the dumpster next to me that smells like used kitty litter. "I want to marry her, Landon."

He stills, and his mouth opens like he's not sure whether to be shocked or pick me up and throw me in the kitty litter dumpster. "You're getting married?"

I hold my hands up. "No! I haven't asked her. I haven't even told her I love her yet. But she's it, man. She's the only woman I can see myself with, and I want it to be endgame. I want her sitting next to me on an old porch swing and letting me massage her old lady feet while our grandchildren run around the yard. I love her." I look at the ground and catch my breath. "Don't take that away from me. Don't take *her* away from me with your disapproval. She loves you and will listen to you."

"If it's real with you, she won't listen to me. I'm just her brother."

"You two have been thick as thieves as adults. She'll listen to whatever you have to say."

He cusses under his breath and turns to the alley door. "Way to fuck up our friendship."

"Why does it have to fuck up our friendship?" I ask.

He spins back around. "You think we can ever pick up women again?"

"Bro, I don't want to pick up another woman for the rest of my life. You haven't listened to a thing I've said. She's it. No more wingman. No more team pickups. It doesn't mean we can't be friends."

"It's weird for me. I mean..."

"What?" I ask, straining to listen and waving toward my ear so I can hear what he has to say. "What's weird?" I ask, panting.

"Dude, we've...you know. We've shared before. I've watched you fuck one end of a girl while I took the other. Remember Taylor Jones? It's weird if you'll be my brother-in-law someday."

A laugh escapes my chest, and some of my blood sprays on Landon's shirt. He looks at it and frowns. "We didn't exactly know we were going to be brothers-in-law during our youth, and I know for a fact I'll never have to worry about my best friend having an affair with my wife."

"You're fucking gross, you know that?" he asks as a smile creases the corners of his mouth.

"Landon, I need a rag, and I'm desperately in need of some ice. I think your hand also needs ice because my face is tougher than we thought. Let's go in the bar and get some ice, grab a beer, and handle this like men."

"I thought we just did."

"We handled it like boys...like the little boys we've been acting like for years. Now it's time to act like men. That means you smiling and being my best man when I eventually marry your sister and us going into the bar and icing ourselves."

He blows out a breath, and his shoulders slouch. "Fine. But you're buying, asshole."

"Dickhead."

"Sister fucker."

"Hey, she's not *my* sister," I say as Landon holds the door open for me and pushes me through the door a little harder than necessary.

Revelations

LANEY

"I'll kill him. Why'd he do this to you? Where is he?" I fire off the questions and don't give Milo a chance to answer as I adjust a bag of frozen peas on the bridge of his nose.

"It's fine. We had a beer. We didn't talk when we drank it. We both just iced ourselves and drank in silence. When we got home, he took off. Said he needed to drive. It's fine, Laney." He looks at me and blinks through his swollen face. "He knows now. We can see what happens. I wish we could have told him together, but it didn't happen that way."

He reaches for me, and I slink onto his lap, wrapping my arms around his shoulders. He winces a little, and I back off, not fully sinking into his beaten body.

"I'm going to take a shower and wash everything. I might feel better. Want to join me?"

I slide right back off his lap and think for a moment. "Get started, and I'll come up in a few minutes. I want to write out a short note to Landon so he'll see it when he gets home. He's not answering my texts."

Milo leans over me and kisses me lightly on the cheek. "Don't take too long, or I really will get started without you." He presses my hand to his pants, and I see what he means.

"It'll be a short note."

He smiles and bounds up the stairs to his bathroom as I huff out a sigh and set about his living room area to look for a pen, smiling to myself the whole time.

Landon won't ruin this. I won't let him. After all these years, Milo and I are dating, and Landon's just going to have to live with it. I'll write him a note, stick it on his door, and tell him we need to have an adult conversation without him hitting Milo or dragging Milo's name through the dirt.

If I could only find a fucking pen. Do they not have such things in this house? Not a pen in sight on the tables, the kitchen counter, or even on the small desk in the corner. I know everyone texts to communicate, but not one pen?

Tentatively, I open the top drawer of the desk and rifle through it. Nothing but a pack of thank you cards that my mother gave Landon in the hopes of giving him good manners, a staple remover, and an old pack of discontinued gum.

I open the drawer below it and hit pay dirt. A package of ballpoint pens sits unopened on top of other odds and ends, and I pick the package up, ready to tear it open and steal a pen. Surely, Milo and Landon won't care that I opened it.

As I fight with the plastic wrapping on the package, a yellow envelope catches my eye. It's face down and under where I just grabbed the package of pens. I cock my head to the side and stare at the back of it.

It's the same type of envelope I mail my panties in. Size. Shape. Color. It's all the same.

I shouldn't look. Maybe it's mail to Milo. Is it a federal crime to look at what it is if it's already out of the mailbox and sitting in the desk drawer? Sure, it's snooping, but my curiosity is peaked.

With a trembling hand, I flip the envelope over and gasp. I gasp before my brain can even process the full extent of what I'm seeing. This is no blank envelope. It's an envelope addressed to a box in Wisconsin with the name Billy Shitner on it.

Billy Shitner. Billy Shitner. I know I'm in deep poop here, but the name still spins in my head like it's ping-ponging into a coherent thought. The sound of the shower runs upstairs, and I panic as it reminds me where I am.

Dear God. Is Milo Billy Shitner?

That's the best option here, and the only one I'll accept. The other option is that my brother is Billy Shitner, but I cannot even entertain that thought. It has to be Milo. Memories stack upon each other and rush back to me - all the questions about my side gig, if I have enough money, and Milo being embarrassed and awkward when we started working together.

He's been paying for and playing with my panties all along, even before I let him play with my panties when I'm wearing them.

Heat and shame blossom in my chest. How did he find out? What must he think of me?

Footsteps on the stairs don't faze me. I don't let go of the pens, and I don't drop the envelope. I'm still frozen in place when Milo, wrapped in a towel I'd normally love to peel away from his body, appears on the stairs. He swirls his hips and twerks. "Laney, are you coming up? The water's..." His voice trails off when he sees what I'm holding. His eyes open wide, and the smile disappears from his face in slow motion.

The envelope falls from my hands, and I don't pick it up. We both stare at it for a few moments, unable to look at each other. "I was looking for something to write with." My voice is weak. "I found more than a pen."

I finally tear my eyes away from the envelope and force myself to look at him. He doesn't look back. He blinks a few times, and I know he's searching for words. "Are you Billy Shitner?"

"Laney, I can explain." His voice is low and husky, almost a whisper.

"Are you Billy Shitner?" I yell. My face crumples, and I spin around the room, gripping my hair because I have no idea what to do with my hands. Strangle him? Take a few swings at him so I can hit the spots my brother missed? Fling open the door and run, not stopping until I reach Guatemala?

He walks down the last few stairs, still gripping the wet towel at his waist. "Laney, it's not what you think."

"Who told you?" I yell, unable to control my voice. I can't decide if I'm mad at him or mad at myself. Probably both. He stares at me like he's never seen me before. He's never seen me yell at him or anyone else, so it could be a shock. "How do you fucking know?"

"I overheard Chantel and Samantha," he says, holding his hands up like I'm robbing him.

I back toward the door and blindly reach for my purse, shaking my head and letting tears fall from my eyes. I don't try to stop them. Shame. I've never felt shame like this.

"Don't go," Milo says, reaching his hand out in front of him and crossing the room in a few steps until he's standing in front of me, water once again dripping down his perfect body. His hands are on my shoulders, and it's the first time I feel nothing when he touches me. "Don't leave like this. Don't leave me."

Don't leave him? Am I still his to leave? After what he knows, why does he want me to stay?

What do I say to that? Whatever the correct answer is here, I don't know it. Millions of comebacks rattle their way through my brain at once, and my head hurts.

My heart hurts more because it's breaking into a million pieces.

"Laney, words. I need words here, baby. What's going through your mind?"

I shake my head and face the door, my hand already on the brass knob. He puts his hand on the door, blocking me from leaving. His other hand is at my back and running up and down my spine. "Please don't leave like this. Don't be mad. We have something good. I don't want to lose you. Please!"

The huskiness in his voice and the sound of the man I love begging for me not to leave him destroys me.

I take his hand off the door, and I almost can't let go. I force myself to drop his hand even though it feels so right in mine. As embarrassed and pissed off as I am, I still want to hold him. Touch his skin. I just...can't.

"I'm so ashamed, Milo," I sob, opening the door and sprinting for the safety of my car.

Shame

LANEY

"Say it again. Slower this time," Samantha says, signaling the waiter for another shrimp cocktail.

My face is hidden behind my palms, and I don't even put my hands down to accept the pretzel bite Chantel waves in front of my face. "Milo's Billy Shitner," I mumble.

"The guy from *Star Trek*?" Samantha asks.

"That's William Shatner," Chantel helpfully explains so I don't have to. "Billy Shitner is her biggest panty client besides some guy in Idaho named Lloyd Biggins."

"Milo's been buying your panties?" Samantha asks. "I have questions. For example, does Landon know? How long has this been going on?"

I lower my hands and open my mouth for the pretzel bite. Chantel pops it into my mouth with a satisfied look and picks up another. She dips the new piece in the beer cheese that came with the appetizer and waves it in front of my face again, hopeful I'll eat a second one.

I chew the first one, swallow, and think. "I don't think Landon knows. He'd probably kill Milo instead of just taking a couple of shots at him. As for how long it's been going on, I guess a couple months or so. Maybe a little longer. A couple weeks before Milo and I..." My voice fades away as tears well up in my eyes, and my throat constricts until I make a gagging noise.

Samantha practically pounces on the shrimp as soon as the waiter places it on the table. She takes a large pink piece and dips it into the cocktail sauce before smiling as she chews. "The fact that you've been fucking Milo Coulson and didn't tell us is enough to shock the hell out of me. This is a lot to throw at us, you know?"

"I knew," Chantel says, raising her hand. "Well, I just learned recently."

"I'm so sorry for upsetting you," I say sarcastically, taking a drink of the martini I've been craving and can finally afford from selling my panties to Milo. I better enjoy it because I'm never selling another pair of panties on that infernal site. Lloyd Biggens will have to live without my white lacy goodies, too.

I'm ashamed, embarrassed, triggered, and...well, I'd need a thesaurus to come up with another word for what I'm feeling. I want the universe to open a hole so it can suck me into some infinite vortex like that sand creature in *Return of the Jedi*.

I've been sharing intimate moments with Milo for weeks and completely oblivious to the fact that my dirty, shipped panties were loitering somewhere in his apartment. I never saw any when I was over there. Where did he hide them so I wouldn't see? His closet? I would borrow a shirt every so often, so that would be too dangerous. I could look in his drawers at any moment. The basement? A good choice since Landon never went down there. Did Milo go down there, move dusty boxes aside, and giggle to himself as he fondled my underwear?

God, the filth of it. How did he look at me the way he did for the last couple of months? I'm gross and foul.

At least I know what he was hiding when we texted that night. Were the infinite dots him trying to tell me he was buying my panties on the Internet?

"Let's calm down about this and look at it rationally," Samantha suggests, dipping a shrimp in cocktail sauce and holding it out for me.

I lean forward, open my mouth, and let my friend feed me like I'm a toddler or a baby bird. "Rationally? There's nothing rational about this. I'm fucked. He'll probably tell everyone at work. He'll never want to see me again. My mother will wonder why he doesn't come around anymore. I'll be responsible for my entire family never seeing him again."

Samantha wipes her lips with her napkin and glares at me. "First, he's known for a couple of months and he never outed you at work. Does he take the panties to work and show them to coworkers at a board meeting?"

I shrug. "Not that I know of, but the way my year is going, I'm not counting anything out."

"He's not going to fuck with your job. Besides, he cares about you and knows how much you need it. In fact, have you given any thought to the fact that buying your panties was his way of helping you financially?"

I straighten my shoulders, remembering the times Milo begged me to let him loan me money or pay for something. He's always wanted to provide for me, even when I was a teen. The ice cream truck. The random snow cone. I also remember him stepping in and paying for my skate rental when Dad only gave me enough cash for the admission fee. Even when we dated, he'd want to pay the full check or that admission to the basketball game. I refused any of his help. We fought over the check, and he routinely found a waitress in the middle of a meal and asked the check be handed directly to him, even if it was a chain restaurant.

"Second," Samantha continues, ticking her points off her fingers. This is turning into a lecture. "Did he ask you to stay and work it out?"

"Well, yes," I mumble.

"He definitely wants to see you again. He's known all along and wasn't turned off. If anything, it sounds like you've been fucking like rabbits. Is it possible it turned him on?" Her face lights up and her eyes widen. "What if this is what made him make a move on you? I mean, you've known each other for years and nada." She slaps the table, and Chantel and I both startle. "He buys your panties and all of a sudden he's asking to spend time with you and giving you millions of orgasms? Coincidence? I think not."

"You're saying it wasn't me that enticed him but it was my Bucky's Bargain Bin stash of underwear that was the catalyst for the best relationship, as short-lived as it was, of my adult life? Way to make me feel worse!"

"Those must have been some special panties," Chantel whispers, sipping her drink. Samantha and I ignore her.

"As for your family, any feelings you have about this come second. You chose to sell the panties. Sure, he found out about it and bought them, but he shouldn't lose your family or his friendship with your brother over it. At the end of the day, you chose to sell. He chose to buy. This stays between you and Milo. It doesn't involve your dad."

"Unless her dad is really Lloyd Biggins. What are the chances?" Chantel adds. "Plot twist."

"Shut up, Chantel," Samantha and I say at the same time.

Samantha continues, "Whatever happened with you and Milo, you both knew there was a possibility it could flame out. You can't bring your family into this. If you run into Milo at your grandmother's funeral someday, you're going to put your big girl panties on, for lack of a better term, and you're going to smile."

I know she's right. It's the adult thing to do.

It'll just be *really* hard. How can I smile and hug Milo like nothing's wrong or nothing ever happened between us when I run into him? How can I be in the same room with him without thinking about how hard I came on his tongue?

I open my mouth and Chantel slides another pretzel bite into it. I chew, remembering another part of the confrontation with Mio.

"Incidentally, he said he found out from you two idiots," I say after I swallow.

Samantha and Chantel freeze and look at each other. Samantha turns a shade of red I haven't seen since she walked out of the work bathroom with her skirt tucked in her underwear. "We were worried about that," Samantha eventually says.

"Worried about it? How did you fuck me this badly?"

"It was at that party at Milo's a couple months ago. Chantel and I were in the basement and thought we heard the door at the top of the stairs shut. When we came upstairs, Milo was leaning against the counter and said he didn't see anyone. That must have been when he heard us talking."

"It *has* to be it," Chantel adds. "You're our friend, so we don't make a habit of talking behind your back. We haven't hung out much because, well, it's fucking winter. No cookouts or pickup frisbee games means not talking much. That's the only time I can remember discussing it."

"Did he seem weirded out?" I ask, a tear dangerously close to slipping out of my eye again. I can't help but wonder what Milo thought of their conversation. Was he shocked I'd do something like this? Did he gag at the thought? Wonder how I came up with my username?

I close my eyes and place my head on the table where the wood is cold against my cheek. Chantel and Samantha chat about the conversation in the basement, but I can't concentrate on their words. All I can think about is that Milo knows my username is HeavilySoiled. Will he call me that for the rest of our lives? Every time there's an event, will he ask, "Is HeavilySoiled going to be there?" When I die, will he slip a note in my casket with HeavilySoiled in the greeting?

Samantha pats my back, and I stare at the restaurant wall, not even sure what to say to my friends.

"I don't think he'll let this go, Laney. He loves you," Samantha says.

"I've been telling her that since she told me she was seeing him and she wondered why I wasn't surprised. He's always loved her." Chantel sniffs like she knows everything. "He'll want to talk this out."

"I doubt it." I groan a little and press my forehead against the table. Once my friends can't see me, I let the tear on my eyelid drop to my lap. "He's probably off getting drunk as shit with my brother, picking up some beautiful woman to mesmerize with his mouth, and regretting ever talking to me."

Double Shame

MILO

"What the fuck is wrong with you?" Landon asks from somewhere behind me. I can't be sure where he is exactly because the entire room spins and people around us are big, blurry blobs. I only recognize his voice. "Is this because I kicked your ass?"

My eyes finally focus, and Landon's concerned face appears. I may not be able to see anyone else in the bar, but I can feel them. Stares. Eyes on the back of my head and on Landon. I'm sure I'm a sight with my fucked-up face, tears in my eyes, my hair askew, and the smell wafting from my pores can't be pleasant.

"How did you find me?" I ask. At least, I think that's what I said. I'm slurring more than a little.

Landon waves his hand in front of his face. "Dude, the bartender texted me half an hour ago and said you were toast. You're lucky I'm friends with Madison enough for her to contact me. How did you think you were going to get home?"

"I couldn't call my best friend," I taunt. Landon scowls at me like I kicked him in the nuts. "All you're good for is kicking my ass, apparently."

He sighs and puts his hands on his hips. "I thought we worked this out. Christ, we went back into the bar and had a beer. What the fuck? Why did you decide to be butthurt about a few love slaps *now*?"

I shake my head and growl like one of the drunk old men you see in movies. Great. I'm the stereotypical sloshed man that scares people.

"Did something happen with Laney?" Landon asks. He leans over me and quickly retreats when he smells the tequila.

I lift my head, and tears spill down my bruised cheeks. "Not a good day with the Wyatts."

Landon pulls out the bar stool and sits down. He waves Madison over and speaks words I can't understand. She soon hands him my debit card, and Landon grabs my wrist, moving my hand to sign the bar ticket. We look so much like a ventriloquist and his dummy that I chuckle.

"Why are you laughing?" Landon asks. "I see nothing funny about having to help my buddy sign his bar tab of...holy shit, Milo. You spent $150.19 on liquor in the last couple of hours?"

"Wow. That's a new record."

"I wouldn't be proud of that $150."

"You forgot the nineteen cents," I say, my head hitting the bar again.

Landon grips my shoulders and pulls me to an upright position. He gestures to Madison to bring me a glass of water and holds me up by the back of my shirt. "Spill it. I just kicked your ass because I was afraid you were going to fuck over my sister." He checks his watch. "Three hours. How did you fuck her over three hours after you assured me you wouldn't?"

"What makes you think I was the one that fucked up?"

"Laney doesn't fuck up."

That's the damn truth. I'm the one that shit the bed here. Why did I keep the envelope? Why did I even continue to buy her underwear after I knew what she tasted and smelled like? Once we started dating, I should have burned all the panties or thrown them in a bag and tossed them into an alley dumpster in another town. I should have limited my purchases to one pair.

I'm a fucking moron, and this is all my fault.

"Are you going to kill me if I did something really fucked up?"

Landon scowls. "How bad we talking?"

I take a deep breath through my nose and immediately wish I hadn't. I smell so bad I can't stand myself. "The kind where I bought your sister's dirty underwear off that site Samantha jokingly suggested and then she found out I was buying her panties. That kind of bad," I finish, squinting one eye because I'm waiting for the punch.

Landon cracks his knuckles and sets his jaw to a more pissed-off expression than I saw a few hours ago when he kicked my ass the first time. He lets go of my shirt, and I slump back to the bar with a thud. Thankfully, I'm so drunk that I don't feel it. If there will be a bruise there, I can add it to the list.

His punch never comes, though.

"She sold her underwear on that site? I thought that was a joke."

"Ha! Joke's on both of us assholes," I slur back, momentarily raising my head and smiling at him like a lunatic. "She made an account. I overheard the girls talking about it in the basement. I bought a pair."

After I say the words, I realize how asinine the story sounds. He probably has no idea what basement or what girls I'm talking about.

"Let me understand," he says, grabbing a handful of bar pretzels from one of the bowls. "Not only have you fucked my sister, which you already got your ass kicked for, but you bought her dirty panties on a skeezy website.”

“I did it to protect her.”

He laughs. “Protect her? From what?”

“From other men buying them. I did a service to your family,” I say, straightening my shoulders and accepting the water in front of me. “I protected her honor.”

“And you didn’t look at them or touch them, right? You just put them under your bed or something, still in the envelope.”

I chuckle. “Hell no. I jerked off with them and used them as wash-cloths. Come on, man. Get real. What would you do with your dream girl’s underwear?”

He grits his teeth but still doesn’t throw a punch at me. “I’d keep them in an envelope and give them back to her like a respectful gen-tleman. Even better, I wouldn’t buy them at all. I’d offer to help her if she was in financial trouble.”

I slap the bar, and patrons around us jump. The bartender startles and sloshes beer down a glass. “Have you met Laney?”

“We came out of the same uterus. I’m familiar with her.”

“I’ve offered. Fuck, man, I offered the night she got fired! You heard me. Your sister’s so stubborn and prideful that she won’t accept help from anyone. Hell, I couldn’t even pay for her ticket to a basketball game. Any time we went out for lunch, she paid for her own, never allowing me to look in the direction of the check. I had the wait staff bring me the check when we had dinner, but I had to arrange it like it was a fucking CIA mission by pretending I had to go to the bathroom and tracking down a waiter or host. I tried, Landon. I tried a million times. I just...wanted to help her. Sure, I had my own lusty motives for buying her panties, and those were fun, but they were always secondary to making sure she had food in the fridge and gas in the tank. I swear to fucking God."

I look at him in my peripheral vision, still scared to make eye contact, lest he be like a cornered wolf and consider that a challenge. But his face softens. He knows his sister, and he knows I tried.

I tried so fucking hard. I'd give her the world if I could.

He sighs, pinching the bridge of his nose. "My mother is the same."

"Your mother sells her dirty underwear? How did I miss her account?"

"Watch your tone, dickhead." He smiles at my shitty joke despite himself.

"How did your father win her over enough for your mother to agree to be a stay-at-home mom when you were little?"

"He didn't ask permission to provide for her. Kind of like how you cornered the wait staff. He paid the bills and put the grocery money in her account so it was there when she was at the checkout lane. He never asked. He just...did. After a couple of years, she got the hint and saw how much he enjoyed providing for his family. She stayed at home, saved a shit ton on daycare expenses, and then went back to work when she was ready. Eventually, the roles reversed, as you know. Dad got such bad arthritis, he couldn't sit at a desk like he did for years, so he retired early. She supported him. Don't get me wrong, she called the shots in her life and made her own decisions before Dad had to retire, but he wanted it easier for her." He sighs and shakes his head at the memory. "It was always like he was a football player protecting his quarterback, pushing any obstacles out of the way so she could run the ball. That's what true partnership is. Him working to make her happy. Her picking up the ball and running it when he couldn't anymore."

He looks in the mirror behind the bar, and I follow his line of sight, grimacing when I see my reflection. Even if there were no embarrassing panty purchases, my reflection is enough to make Laney run away.

"Both of the Wyatt women are stubborn as donkeys," he says. He runs his hand through his hair. "It doesn't mean you can't help. When you see something, take the initiative."

"Take the initiative," I mumble under my breath, nodding.

Landon stares in the mirror as I sip my water. He shoves the pretzel bowl in my direction, indicating I need something to sop up the alcohol, and I don't argue. We reach into the bowl periodically, nibbling in silence until both the bowl and my water glass are empty.

Landon slaps me on the back. "Let's get home so you can sober up. We'll work out a solution to help you get her back tomorrow."

I meet his eyes, and my mouth opens in surprise. "You're going to help me?"

"I hate the idea of you and my sister, but what I hate more is the possibility of my sister with a guy who doesn't care about her nearly as much as you obviously do. You took a hell of a beating tonight. Physically and emotionally. Looking at it now, I don't think I can watch my sister get married to another guy who *doesn't* worry about her to the point of buying all her panty stock when she needs money. I'd hate him. I'd despise him for you, bro."

I stand and immediately wobble. Landon grabs my shirt again and holds me as I lean against the bar, getting my feet under me. The bartender and patrons around us sigh in relief that I'm leaving. I must be a wreck.

"Thanks, Landon. I'm going to get her back. Not tonight, obviously."

"Probably not tomorrow the way I think your hangover is going to go. Better call in to work."

I stick my finger in the air like I invented something profound. "But someday! I'll win your sister back, so help me God!"

Landon turns me in the direction of the door. "You have another ass kicking coming over the underwear," Landon says, getting his keys out of his pocket and swinging my arm over his shoulder to help me out the door. "Don't think I'm going to let you off the hook just yet for that. I'll give your face the chance to heal a little first, though."

"You're a regular Mother Teresa, Landon Wyatt."

Grand Gestures

LANEY

I haven't eaten a thing. The ramen noodles stare back at me from the cooling bowl. I even tried adding chopsticks and half a boiled egg on top to make it more like fancy restaurant ramen. No such luck. I still don't want to eat them. They're limp and unappetizing.

I showered today, which I consider a win since I haven't showered for the last three days. I haven't gone to work, talked to anyone, or done any life maintenance during my campaign to be as gross as possible and remove myself from any social activities popular with my generation. I haven't been out of the house since dinner with Samantha and Chantel.

Fuck my bills. Fuck my loans. Fuck being clean and well-shaved. I'll just sit here and rot on the couch, talking to nobody but myself. I'll be one of those people who talks to inanimate objects like walls and stuffed animals. Chantel will have to evict me, but I'll permanently attach myself to the couch. Movers she hires will have to pick up the couch and set it in the yard with me still on it like a bad urine stain after a drunken night out.

Until that day comes, I'll stay here, watching old episodes of *Judge Judy*.

A knock at the door interrupts Judy's judgment, and I turn up the volume. I refuse to move. Refuse to let even the mailman see me in my agony and shame. I don't want to see anyone ever again.

Another knock.

"I don't have any packages coming, and I don't need pest control services," I yell. "Spiders are our friends. I know Jesus, so unless you have cookies, you can fuck right off." I pause and think. "Actually, I can't afford the cookies, either."

And I can't now that I'm not selling my dainties.

"What if I have flowers?"

Cold dread moves down my back like an ice cube. I know that voice. "Milo?" I yell back.

"Laney, please answer the door."

"No." I say it deadpan. It's just not happening. I can't face him.

There's silence on the other side of the door. "Please," he says just when I think he must have left.

The way he said it wasn't a request or his light-hearted voice telling me to suck it up and open the door. It was pleading. Begging.

I sit up and stretch, realizing I haven't used my muscles in days. I sniff my armpits and quickly pull my hair into a high ponytail before brushing cracker crumbs from my shirt. On the way to the door, I backtrack several times until I'm sure he will have given up and left. I turn the knob and swing the door open only a crack, finding Milo on the porch, a bouquet of flowers in his hand.

Seeing him takes my breath away, but it's not in the way he normally leaves me breathless. He's pale, and dark circles shadow his eyes. The bruises from my brother's fists have faded to a light yellow. His hair is messy like usual, but it doesn't seem as stylish. It looks like he rolled out of bed, threw his messenger bag over his broad chest, and came over. It's, well, it's not like him at all. But his clothes are clean, and I catch a whiff of fresh soap and shampoo. He has me beat there.

"Can I come in?" he asks.

"Are those peonies? Why peonies and not roses or daisies? Lillies?" I don't know why that's the first thing out of my mouth.

"Peonies sound like panties when you say it fast, so I was hoping I could make you laugh."

Before I can control my mouth, my damn lips betray me, and the corners of my mouth lift. I cover them with a fist like I'm holding in a cough, but Milo's already caught me, a smile on his own face. "Please, Laney. I just want to talk."

I back away from the door and leave it open. He steps into my house and immediately fills the entire room with...Milo. He could always fill a room, and part of me is glad that hasn't changed.

But *we've* changed.

He holds out the flowers, and I take the bouquet, even sniffing it and savoring the smell before walking to the kitchen and putting them in an old jelly jar. Once I'm back in the living room, I wave him to the couch, and he sits on one end as I slink onto a cushion at the opposite side. We look like an angry married couple on the verge of divorce as we sit on the marriage therapy couch. I cross my legs and stare out the window in front of me, not meeting his eyes.

He clears his throat. "I'm sorry," he says, barely speaking above a whisper. "I can't imagine how you must feel."

"No, you can't. To do that, you'd have to reach rock-bottom so that you have to sell your underwear to strangers, only to find out the person you want most in the world has been buying them all along."

Out of my peripheral vision, I see him turn his head to me. "I'm the person you want most?"

I snort. "Go ahead and act like you have no idea."

"I'm not acting. I really have no idea what's going through your mind right now. Talk to me."

I get up from the couch and pace. He watches with calm, calculating eyes. Is he thinking of his next words? A better way to reassure me that the world doesn't think less of me?

"I'm humiliated, Milo. My dirty underwear, for fuck's sake. The smell of it alone...Christ."

"I've smelled and tasted every part of you since we started doing whatever it is we're doing. Why are you embarrassed that I smelled your panties?"

"I...I just am! I don't need to rationalize it to you. I feel so fucking betrayed. Why did you do that? Were you trying to humiliate me before you fell for me? Was it a gag on your best friend's sister? A prank you thought was funny?" I'm yelling now, and I hate that I'm yelling at Milo Coulson.

"God damn it, Laney. It's not like that!" He yells right back at me, jabbing a finger at his chest. "Yeah, I was curious at first. I wanted to know what you smelled like. What you tasted like. I've been obsessed with you for years. I bet you didn't know that. Yes, it was a borderline creepy obsession. I was so frustrated, sweetheart. I was frustrated because you're my best friend's little sister, and I couldn't have you. It was not a joke or a prank. You were off limits. So...I made love to your underwear. Is that what you want to hear?"

"Most certainly not! I can honestly say that I've never wanted to hear those words from a man."

"Well, I did. I put them on my face and inhaled every particle of scent I could, and I fantasized about you riding my mouth. OK?

Happy? I even hooked a pair over my ears like it was a fucking face mask." Milo mimes attaching something to his ears. "After that, I used your underwear as a washcloth when I jerked off in the shower. I hear the words coming out of my mouth and realize how fucked up they are! I do. That's what I did. At least, that's what I did at first."

"What do you mean?"

"After the initial curiosity was over and we were together, I kept buying them because I wanted to help you, and I personally couldn't wrap my puny caveman brain around another guy buying your panties and doing what I was doing with them. I wanted to buy your stock so other people wouldn't."

"You did this because you were jealous of Lloyd Biggins from Idaho?"

Milo looks at me and blinks. "Who the *fuck* is Lloyd Biggins from Idaho?"

"My other big buyer."

"Holy shit. You have another big buyer?" He puts his head between his legs. "I'm going to throw up."

I slide down the wall and sit on the floor, my legs splayed out in front of me like I don't have the heart to move. I don't. I'm exhausted.

"I love you," he says, his head still between his legs. I lift my head like I don't understand his words. "I have for a long time. I just want you to know that. I love you. Fuck me to hell and back, but I love you, Laney. I don't love you like my best friend's little sister. I love you because you're everything I want in a woman." He sniffs loudly. "If you never talk to me again, I understand." He shakes his head between his legs, and a tear falls from his hidden face onto my carpet.

"I have everything a man could want in life except the one person I want at my side. What I did was fucked up beyond all reason. Creepy. Stalkerish. Downright fucking cringey. I get it. But please believe I did it because I want you. I guess, in the back of my mind, I was close to you when I held your panties in my hand, and it was the only way I could be close to you then. It was sick and wrong."

He raises his face, and tears sting my eyes to see the tears filling his. How can he still affect me like this?

"Milo." I don't know what to say. I can only squeak out his name. It's the name of the man I love.

"I'll spend the rest of my life making it up to you if you let me. So help me fucking God."

The rest of my life? Does that mean what I think it means?

"You want to talk about shame? I'm the only one that should be ashamed here. I found out about you selling your underwear and instead of ignoring it and letting you handle your business, I acted like a dipshit and bought them. I did dirty shit with your underwear. Laney, I used your underwear for some dirty needs I have. I'm the one that should be ashamed."

He inhales and wipes his face before reaching into his messenger bag and pulling out a plastic store carrier. "Here," he says, dumping out the contents of the bag onto my coffee table. Fabric rains from the bag – black lace, white cotton, red polyester crap. It's like the underwear bargain bin was dumped onto my furniture.

"This is all of them. I washed, dried, and folded them. They're clean. If you want them ironed, I'll do that. If nothing else, you have a lifetime supply of panties. I just wanted you to have them back." He clears his throat. "This and the flowers, it's what I can do, Laney. I mean, there's no greeting card that says 'Sorry I bought your dirty underwear and jerked off to them.'" He smiles a wry grin. "But now that I think about it, that may be an untapped market. Lloyd Biggins may need a card like that someday."

I don't laugh at his stupid joke. I wipe my eyes like a big girl and push off the floor, flinging myself toward the couch so fast that he covers his face, probably expecting me to make it a full week of Wyatt ass-kicking and take a swing at him. But my arms wrap around his neck, and I pull him into me, deeply inhaling the masculine scent of his soap. Him.

After he realizes I'm not going to hit him, he strokes my hair. "Laney, I love every part of you. Don't push me away over this."

"I know," I say. I take a deep breath, mentally saluting that four-teen-year-old girl who found Milo standing in our kitchen with an open container of ice cream, a smile, and perfect abs. If she only knew we'd get the guy in the end. "I've loved you for so long that I don't even know when it began, Milo."

He sniffs and pulls back, cupping my cheek. A tear rolls down my face, and he swipes it away with his thumb. "You love me?"

I laugh. "Of course, I love you, you fucking bastard. I've loved you for far longer than you've loved me. Don't act like you're special here."

"Why did you leave me then?" he asks, clutching his chest like his heart hurts.

"Because I love you so much that I was so embarrassed that you saw me broke and low and selling my panties to strangers on the Internet. I'm ashamed..." My voice trails away as my face crumples, my chin quivering so hard that my lips won't move. He holds my face so I can't turn away, though. "You saw me like that. You saw my...lowest."

"I'm the only person in this room that should be ashamed. And I am. But can we move past it? For us?"

"How the fuck do you think we'll accomplish that?"

He chuckles and a little snot comes out his nose. Neither one of us really care. "I've seen your underwear a lot over the last few weeks. I didn't even have to pay for it. You have nothing to be ashamed of,

Laney." My eyes look down, and he tilts my face so I have to look at him again. "You support yourself to the point where you infuriate me with your stubbornness. I want to provide things for you. Protect you. Let me, Laney. It's what I need from us. I *need* to protect and provide for the woman I love. Something. I'm not asking you to be at home, barefoot and pregnant. But let me buy you dinner without making it a big deal. Let me buy you a pair of earrings I know you want. *Let me.*"

"That's such a patriarchal idea."

"Shit, Laney," he mutters before his lips meet mine.

It's a hungry kiss, and he devours my mouth, moving his tongue against my teeth until I give up the fight and open my lips further for him.

I was always going to give up the fight with him. I surrender. Milo Coulson wins.

His hands are under the hem of my shirt and lifting the fabric over my head before I know what's happening. His head dips to my cleavage, and he trails whisper kisses across the trembling flesh there. "Do you want to know what I did to your panties, Laney? Do you want me to show you?"

"Show me everything," I whisper, no longer caring that he was Billy Shitner all along. If he doesn't care or I wasn't diminished in his sight, I shouldn't let it bother me. This is my Milo.

My Milo. Forever.

He picks me up and lifts me off the couch as I wrap my legs around him, my lips never leaving his. At this point, a nuclear blast couldn't separate us.

The front door opens, and Chantel stomps into the room, shaking snow from her boots and stopping short when she catches Milo carrying me and sees me topless. "Oh, my," she says, the cold air coming through the door with her. "Don't mind me."

We don't. We don't even speak to her. Milo carries me right past her, heading for the stairs and not caring that my hands frantically grip the back of his shirt like I can't get it off his body fast enough.

He kicks the door to my room closed and doesn't bother locking it. I'm pretty sure Chantel knows not to come in for the next hour unless she wants a show. He places me on my bed, and we finally break our kiss as I scramble back to rest my head on the pillows.

Milo stays at the foot of my bed and unbuckles his pants, his eyes dark and dangerous. "Slide your panties down those beautiful legs."

"W-why?"

"I told you I was going to show you what I did with them, and a promise is a promise, sweetheart."

I unbutton my jeans and slide them down with my panties in one movement. I pull the white cotton panties, popular with grandmothers the world over, out of the denim and hold them out for Milo as I stare at his stiff cock, my mouth suddenly watering.

If he's turned off by the huge underwear, he doesn't show it. He pulls his shirt off with a smirk and takes the panties from me. "I'd always start with smelling them. Has anyone ever told you that you smell like waffle syrup?"

"I can't say that I've heard that before."

"After I inhaled your scent, I'd usually lick them. Just a little. Just enough to know how you tasted before I even tasted you for the first time." He darts his tongue out, holds my underwear gusset flat, and stares at me, our eyes locking, as he drags his tongue up the wet fabric. My mouth drops open at the sheer filth and irreverence of it.

When he's licked his way up to the waistband, he smiles an evil grin. "After I smelled and tasted them, I'd wrap them around my dick and rub my cock to them. I liked just feeling something against my dick that had been next to your skin."

"Oh. My. Fucking. God."

"Do you want me to work my dick with your underwear while you watch, Laney?"

"Yes," I whisper, my own fingers itching to rub my clit. I'm desperate for him, and my chest heaves with want.

"Open your legs and let me see that pretty slit while I do it. As soon as I'm close, I'm going to dive into you, lick your pussy clean, and then fuck you senseless until you beg for me to stop. Clear?"

"Uh-huh." It's not eloquent, but it's the only sound I can make.

Our eyes lock as he fists my panties in one hand, grabs my ankle, and pulls me down a little so he can stroke my leg with his other hand. Before he does anything, he drops a line of spit onto his dick, and I watch the line of drool pool at the base of his length. Then, he wraps the white fabric around his cock, breathes in, and cusses as he pumps his dick. "Fuck, Laney. I was so undone by your damn cotton underwear."

He stands at the foot of my bed, his eyes dark and hooded, and jerks his dick with my panties as I watch, saliva pooling under my tongue. I know men masturbate, but watching him as he experiences an intimate moment with his own hand has me undone. "Milo," I moan, my hand coming to my own slit.

My clit throbs under my touch, and Milo growls at me. He shifts his hips as he bucks into my granny panties, and his hand shakes around my ankle.

Eventually, he can't take it anymore, and he throws my panties over his shoulder. I hear them hit the floor behind him with a soft plop, and Milo attacks me.

There's really no other word for it.

He spreads my legs, looks up at me, and practically purrs as he moves my hand out of the way with his nose and wraps his mouth over my clit.

My back bows off the bed, and I wrap my legs over his shoulders as his palms come to my breasts. "You taste better than the panties," he says from between my legs before resuming his suction on my most intimate part. His tongue slides down my center, rims my pussy, and dips to the part of my body between my pussy and my asshole. He stops just before running his tongue over my puckered hole, but that's only because I want his mouth on my clit, and I pull him back to it by the hair of his head.

"I want you right here, Milo."

He smiles against my slit and lightly flicks his tongue once over my trembling nub. That's all I need to grip his head, buck into his wet mouth twice, and shatter apart, moaning his name and cussing every bad word I've ever heard or seen in the written form.

He presses against my stomach with one hand as I curl into my orgasm, and the other hand strokes my hips as he continues to lick me until every ounce of pleasure runs its course.

I pull his shoulders up my body and spread my legs even wider for him. I lock my feet around his naked ass and pull him into me, hoping his cock hits home.

It does, and he slides into me like he knows my body better than his own.

"Laney," he whispers, stroking my hair and burying his face in my neck. "I love every inch of you. Every part of you. Even the parts you don't want anyone to see. The shyness and the shame. I love it all."

That's the last full sentence he says as we rock into each other, reveling in the feel of our joined bodies, until Milo groans one last time and whimpers my name against my neck.

Epilogue

MILO - NINE MONTHS LATER

I can't decide if it's stuffy in here, or if it's just me. I pull at the collar of my ugly, ironic snowman sweater and gulp, hoping it will force my mouth to make saliva. Lord knows it feels like cotton no matter how much bourbon I chug from the tumbler in my hand.

It must be me that's overly hot because everyone else is downright joyful at our friend Christmas party this year. Bottles of wine pour freely, a fire crackles in the fireplace of Landon's new condo, and people laugh and smile as conversation buzzes in the room.

Looking around, it almost feels like home – probably because he owned most of the furniture when we lived together. He took it with him. I eye my old couch and remember all the times I fell asleep there while watching football. The picture frames on the mantle are the same ones that decorated the end tables in the condo we shared.

The condo that I kept. It's also the home Laney and I now share. Landon moved out two months ago, and this party is for both Christmas and his housewarming party with an ugly Christmas sweater and pajamas theme. His room still smelled of his soap and cologne when Laney moved her desk and laptop into it, claiming it as her office.

Well, it's *our* office. I moved my desk up there, too, and we work shoulder-to-shoulder on days I work from home.

Laney found a job doing research for a small local law firm with bigger branches throughout the country. Since the research is mostly done online, she only has to go into the Minneapolis branch when there's an important meeting or when she needs to use the law office's extensive law library for something she can't find online. Surprisingly, Wayno came through on that good reference, which probably had more of Samantha's fingerprint on it than Wayno's. Combined with the great reference my company gave her, the firm was happy to get her.

She also agreed to let me help more, giving me what I need in our relationship. She still pays half of the mortgage on our condo, which is comparable to what she paid Chantel, but I pay the utilities. That's helped her get a handle on saving for a new car she desperately needs. She just quit the driving app last month, but it gave her enough money to pay off the school loan and make double the payments on her medical bills for a few months. She should have that paid off by the middle of next year.

I told her that Lloyd Biggins will just have to fuck right off. He's not getting another pair of her filthy panties. Those are only for me.

"Need another drink?" Landon asks, coming up behind me and slapping me on the back. Hard.

It's not just my imagination. He's still a little butthurt and now shows it in silent, passive-aggressive ways. A harder-than-necessary high five during rec league softball this past summer. A hard slap on the back that'll dribble my drink down the front of my pants when we're out at bars. The way he tells it, he's over me having my way with his sister, but he still takes every opportunity to get a cheap shot under the radar.

"I'm good," I say with a smile. Maybe if I don't comment on his back slaps, they'll eventually stop. "I need to slow down."

I pat the small box in my pajama pants pocket, and Landon notices the movement. The outline of my phone is noticeable through the other pocket, and he crinkles his brow. "What's in your pants?"

"My dick," I say with a shrug.

"Huh. I don't remember your dick being shaped like a little box they use to package jewelry."

"It's a new underwear design. It's like a jock strap. Very high tech."

He laughs, and it sounds like his old laugh - booming and moving quickly to his eyes, making them crinkle. He's fake laughed in my presence a lot over the last nine months. Like he's still getting used to the idea that his sister and I are ride or die.

As soon as he stops guffawing, he takes a drink of the beer he's holding and nods at the ring box. "No, really. What did you get her?"

"I thought I'd get your sister some nice earrings for Christmas."

A flush moves up his cheeks. Yeah, he's going to have to get over this real fast. "Earrings, huh? Yeah, you make sure it's earrings."

I tilt my head to the side. "Why just earrings?"

"It's a safe gift."

"Just out of curiosity, if it wasn't earrings, wouldn't you be happy I'm making an honest woman of her? I mean, you did say you wouldn't like anyone else that married her."

"First, just because I acknowledge you're the best for my sister, doesn't mean I really love it. Second, my sister will never be an honest woman," he says with a laugh.

I don't have the heart to agree since I don't want him to punch me in the face for the first time in nine months. His sister's a dirty little minx, and that's part of why I'm going to ask her to marry me tonight.

I'm going to make her mine. Forever. Officially. And I'm going to be hers.

"Landon," I say gently, waiting patiently until his stupid grin slides off his face. He squints and tilts his head. "It's not earrings. I'm going to ask her to marry me. If you want to kill me, make it quick. Do it before the wedding so we don't leave her a sad widow."

He inhales deeply, and his face turns a color red I usually only associate with people who are choking.

"Are you OK?" I ask.

He bends over, putting his hands on his knees and taking deep breaths. He holds up a finger, and I'm momentarily surprised it's not the middle one. "Give me a minute."

"We already had this conversation when you kicked my ass in that alley. This can't be a surprise."

He waves his hands at me like he wishes a genie would come and make me disappear. "Yeah, bro, but that was months ago. I thought you forgot."

"You thought I was going to forget that I want to marry your sister?"

He squeezes his eyes shut and pinches the bridge of his nose. People walk by, carrying their drinks and laughing, until they see Landon bent over and practically wheezing. I wave them away, and they shrug, moving on to the next small group of people or heading to the table to play dice for gifts.

I pat him on the back, rubbing it in large circles. "I love her, and I'll take care of her forever. She'll take care of me right back. She's good at that, you know?"

He nods, still bent over. "I know. I guess I knew it was coming, but I was hopeful you'd break up in a fiery blaze."

I laugh. "If that happened, you'd really kick my ass for hurting your sister. Can't have it both ways."

He straightens, putting his hand on my shoulder, and I take the gesture as a friendly sign until he grips my ugly Christmas sweater and pulls me close enough that I can smell that he's dipped into the vodka-spiked cranberry drink from the punchbowl. "You fuck this up, and that alley incident will be like a field trip to the zoo in comparison."

"Is that a blessing I hear coming from your mouth?"

Before he can answer, delicate arms wrap around my waist, and Landon straightens, pinning a fake smile on his mouth.

"What's going on? Are you two fighting again?" Laney asks, propping her chin on my other shoulder.

"Never," Landon says, letting go of my sweater and smoothing it down to make sure it isn't bunched. "I was just admiring the great knit job on your boyfriend's outfit. Very expensive wool for such an ugly sweater."

"I was just going to come find you," I say out of the corner of my mouth. I nail Landon with a knowing look. "Can I use the back deck for a bit? I want to up the ante on this party for your sister. Excuse us."

He shakes his head like he just got a chill, but he doesn't spill the beans. "OK. Yeah. Fine. Whatever. I'm just going to go puke. Don't mind me."

I walk Laney out the sliding glass door, my hand on her lower back. When we hit the cold air, our breath steams. It makes me think of last winter and how we got together.

We've always been together as friends and second family. Now we're *together*. I have every intention of staying that way.

I face her and clasp her cold hands in mine. She reaches into her pocket for some gloves, and I stop her, shaking my head.

"I can't wear gloves? It's freezing out here. What's going on?" she asks.

"You can put gloves on in a minute, but there's something I have to do."

She tilts her head and furrows her brow, confusion lining her face. "Is this about my Christmas present? If so, I'd like to wait until Christmas morning."

"Christmas is for Christmas. Tonight is for something else."

I kiss her on her cheek and then sink to my right knee in front of her. Reaching into my pocket, it must hit her what I'm doing, and her eyes widen to the size of silver dollars. Her hands cover her mouth.

I take a deep breath. It's now or never, and I'm already on my knee. "Laney, you've been in my life so long that I don't know life without you. Over the past several months, I've realized I don't ever want to be without you. Will you be my wife?"

Her hands move from her mouth to her chest like she's trying to keep her heart in her rib cage. My knee is cold on the hard deck wood, and the smile on my face falters. Is she going to reject me? "Baby?" I plead.

She shakes her head like she's waking up. "Oh, my God. Milo! Of course, I'll marry you. I just...I had to think a minute."

"You had to think about it?"

"No! I mean, I had to process what you were asking." She throws her arms around me and buries her face in my neck. "I've been thinking about this for a long time. I know I want to marry you. I didn't mean I had to think about marrying you. I just..."

I grin and slide the ring onto her ring finger, admiring how it looks on her. Her voice trails away as the platinum band slides over her knuckles. I place a kiss on her warm lips and tuck her hands into my pants pockets to keep them from the cold. Our tongues mingle, and she trembles against my body.

Her body next to mine. Her lips on mine. Me keeping her hands warm. It'll always be like this.

She pulls back and squints at me. "Is that why my brother was so sick?"

"He still likes to imagine I've never touched you and that you'll be a virgin until you die."

"Such a double standard." She bites her lip and presses her forehead to the spot just under my chin. "Incidentally, I just want to make sure we're doing this for the right reasons."

"What do you mean?" I ask.

"Well, if you're doing this for a lifetime supply of panties, you could have just asked. No need for marriage."

I playfully yank her hair and pull her head back so she has to look up at me. "Such sass. You saw the bag. I have enough for life as it is. You want to know why I'm marrying you?"

"To beat Lloyd Biggins to it?"

I shake my head. "OK, that's another reason to add to the list."

She smiles. "Fine, Milo, tell me the real reason."

I shrug and grab her hand, walking her to the door and the warmth of the party inside. There are a lot of people who will be excited to hear our announcement and celebrate with us tonight.

I kiss her hand and thread my fingers through hers. "I had access to the panties. I'm marrying you to do kinky shit with the socks."

THE END

***

Thanks for reading *The Panty Plot*. I appreciate all my readers, and I'd love it if you could leave a star rating or review on your reading platform of choice.

Other books by Tori Ross:
Romantic Comedy-
All I Wank for Christmas
Contact High
The Cuffing Season Contract
Winning the Witch
The Flower Festival Fling

Steamy Contemporary Romance-
Rocks

Travel Romance Novella Series-
Head Over Heels in Hawaii
Loved in Las Vegas
Christmas on the Cruise Ship
Out of Luck in the Outback
Turkey in Tennessee

Romantic Suspense- (Coming soon!)
Copper

Steamy Superhero Romance-

Arson

Thirst

Darkness

Amp

Erotica-

The Caretaker

The Substitute

The Progressive Dinner

Acknowledgements

This book was a tough one. Not because it was structurally difficult but because I wrote *Copper* (out in April 2024) at the same time. Try writing a romantic suspense and a romantic comedy at the same time. It's not for the weak, and I'm immensely proud that I did it. I'm also taking a bit of a break until diving into my next one. (ONE!)

Thank you to my husband. We had fun looking at the popular website where people sell their panties. Thank you to my friend Lisa. There are only so many people in one's life who will listen to this douchery and let me bounce plot points around.

I got a second dog while I was writing this. Big thanks to Murphy for being a fast learner when it comes to not shitting in the house.

I also have two teenagers. If you're a praying person, I appreciate all you can send my way. They're great kids, and they tolerate my cereal for dinner nights when I'm on a roll.

Thank you to the ARC readers and my author friends. I wouldn't be upright without you.

About the Author

Tori Ross is the bestselling and award-winning author of steamy contemporary romance and romantic comedy. Her book, *The Cuffing Season Contract*, won the National Indie Excellence Award for romantic comedy, and she's written several shorts, novellas, full-length books, and serials. When she's not writing, she runs a podcast called *Sitting Here Reading Corn with Tori Ross* and plays pickleball to get out of the house. She lives with her family and two amazing rescue dogs.

9 798987 994535